the girl who...

Andreina Cordani

ATOM

ATOM

First published in Great Britain in 2021 by Atom

1 3 5 7 9 10 8 6 4 2

Copyright © 2021 by Andreina Cordani

The moral right of the author has been asserted.

A CIP catalogue record for this book is available from the British Library.

ISBN 978-0-349-00352-8

Typeset by Hewer Text UK Ltd, Edinburgh
Printed and bound in Great Britain by Clays Ltd, Elcograf S.p.A.

Papers used by Atom are from well-managed forests and other responsible sources.

Atom
An imprint of
Little, Brown Book Group
Carmelite House
50 Victoria Embankment
London EC4Y 0DZ

An Hachette UK Company
www.hachette.co.uk

www.atombooks.co.uk

Prologue

Boyd, before

I'm not following her. Whatever the others say, I'm really not following her. It's just that wherever I go she seems to be there – in the park, the library, the shops. Outside her school. I see her pretty much everywhere.

Anyway, who cares even if I am? I don't mean her any harm, and I like seeing her.

She is there, a way ahead on the High Street – holding her mother's hand and skipping along. Today she is wearing a neat little red coat, the frill of a pretty blue dress poking out from underneath, and legs in multicoloured stripy tights. A gust of wind catches her blonde hair and whips it back to reveal her beaming face looking up at her mum. Her white front teeth are a little too big for her mouth, making a kind of crooked, sparkling smile that sends little daggers of joy flying towards me. She is perfect. She's golden.

Troy thinks I don't deserve a friend like her. He's right.

I press forward, head down again, pulling my hood up out of habit. A middle-aged woman is coming towards me, staring at her phone, heels clipping the pavement faster and faster. The others murmur restlessly.

She's moving too quick for me to get out of her way, so my elbow catches her sleeve and she looks up. It takes a couple of beats for her to react.

I know what she sees: young bloke, hoodie, tatts, can of cider in hand and clearly off my face on something. Her look of fear and disgust lights a flame in me, gives me this drunken mix of shame, then anger, then power.

Troy thinks I should take her phone while she's distracted.

Bart thinks I should shank her, but that my knife isn't good enough, and it probably wouldn't make it through the wool of her coat.

The others pile in with their opinions but we're not going to do anything really, not in the middle of the street with people and cameras everywhere. As the woman scuttles away – her phone clawed protectively against her chest – that hot bitter flow of power she triggered goes in the bank for later.

My focus changes, darts around the faces of the other passers-by. They're pulling their gaze away, drawing back, minding their own business.

They know I'm dangerous.

I love thinking things like that. I don't want normals to hate me, but if they're going to, I'm glad they fear me as well.

Then I catch another glimpse of the golden girl as she disappears around the corner, stripy legs skipping. *She* doesn't hate me or fear me. When she sees me, she smiles and waves like I'm a normal too. She knows what's going on with me, without even having to ask. I'm not a threat, I'm a friend who's always there, I've got her back.

I wonder if I will run into her later, when her mum isn't around to spoil things.

Of course I will.

Chapter 1

Ellie

'She's not my sister.' I'd said it so many times now, I was thinking about having it printed on a T-shirt.

The lady in the restaurant toilets blushed as she looked down, pretending to wash her hands *really* well as she real-ised what she'd said. Of course, I wasn't Leah Stoke's sister; everyone knows what happened to Leah Stoke's sister.

'Oh yes, um . . .' she stammered. 'I mean, please tell your – your *friend*, what an inspiration she is. I read her dad's book. It saw me through a really difficult time.'

'Mm-hmm, of course, yes I will,' I replied, secretly thinking, *as if.* As if I was going to walk back to our table in the corner where the five of us were waiting for our family-size stuffed crust, pretending we actually were a family, and say, 'Hi Leah, just to let you know, you're an *inspiration.*'

When I got back to the table, I genuinely thought about doing it, just to liven up the situation. I'd taken as long as I possibly could in the bathroom in the hope that something approaching a conversation would have started while I was there, but it hadn't worked. I suppose Mum would have said that was my job, being the one who can talk for Britain.

My brother Dylan's eyes were fixed on his plate and he'd slumped backwards on his chair, so his chin almost touched the table. He had his fork stabbed into a bit of pizza crust and was crashing it into another bit of crust, like they were toy cars. Slightly immature for a thirteen-year-old, but the mental torture of this meal had probably set back his development by five years.

David looked like he'd been scrubbed clean for the occasion. He'd clearly had a shave, and his hair had been combed out and rammed behind his ears, so he looked slightly less like a rough sleeper than usual. He was even wearing a tie – a hideous stripy one my mum had bought for him. But he hadn't cracked a proper smile since we'd sat down.

Yes, I know, *I know*, he's been through a lot, it's no wonder he's a serious kind of guy, etc., etc., but you'd think he'd at least try to turn on the charm. Mum had been going on about this dinner for weeks. She'd made Dylan wear proper trousers, frisked me for glitter before we left, and made us keep our phones firmly in our pockets.

Anyone would have thought she was going to announce her engagement. Which, of course, she was. Bless her, she didn't think we knew.

Right now, her eyes were fluttering anxiously between David and his daughter Leah – the vision of loveliness sitting on the other side of him who hadn't said a word all evening.

As usual Leah looked like she had stepped straight off the set of an American soap opera about troubled, rich teens. Her back straight and her perfect face completely still, all poise and cheekbones. Big lashes hooded liquid blue eyes, as she stared down at her bit of pizza like she'd never seen a Meat Feast before.

'You've been a while, Ellie,' Mum said. 'We had to start on the pizza. And I wanted to say something before we all got completely stuck in.' She put down her fork and laid a hand over David's. His hand didn't move, just lay deadened under hers as she squeezed it.

'I guess now is as good a time as any to tell you . . .'

Here it comes. Come on Ellie, happy face, happy face . . .

'David has asked me to marry him, and I've said yes!'

Around the table three sets of teeth flashed in stiff grins of mock delight. Dylan's had bits of pizza in it, Leah's was even and perfect, her smile looked warm, like she was posing at yet another photo shoot. As for me, I went the whole hog and clapped my hands together in delight. 'Wow! That's *brilliant*!'

What an absolute disaster.

It wasn't that I was jealous, or that I somehow wanted my mother all to myself. I had a life of my own, so more quality time with Mum was not top of my to-do list, and I did want her to be happy. But David and Leah weren't going to make anyone happy ever, not even themselves.

Yes, that was a horrible way to think, but I couldn't help wishing Mum had chosen Mr Average Divorced Man, an every-other-weekend dad with a few hang-ups. Like my friend Gloria's stepdad who was perfectly nice and normal, provided nobody mentioned his ex-wife's name. But that was

Mum for you, the patron saint of lost causes. And you couldn't get any more lost than those two.

Leah was saying something. I vaguely heard 'You've been such a support ... so great ... you're already part of the family...' before I switched off. And so, a moment later, when Mum made her second big announcement, I had to ask her to repeat it.

'I said that we'll be moving into David and Leah's place. You know, over the shop. Ellie, don't look like that, close your mouth.'

I'd been expecting the engagement announcement, but I'd never imagined we'd end up *there*.

'Not the *shop*,' I said.

'It smells funny,' Dylan cut in.

'It just smells of books,' David said defensively. 'And it's a great place to live. You can read anything you want, any time. All that knowledge at your fingertips.'

'Wow, Dave,' I said. 'They should invent something like that for computers. Call it the Cyberwebnet, or something.'

An impatient snort came from Leah. If I had tossed my hair and rolled my eyes like that, Mum would have laughed and called me a little madam, but when Leah did it nobody seemed to notice.

'Come on, Ellie,' Mum said. 'You can't expect David and Leah to give up their home. And it's *David*, remember? Not Dave.' She was staring at me desperately in a don't-ruin-this kind of way, which made me feel really sorry for her. 'You'll have your own room, and you can decorate it any way you like.'

Just for a moment my brain ran off in a different direction, picturing the big mural I'd wanted to paint on my wall for ages, and who I'd get to paint it. I thought about the videos I could make in my new room, what I could do with more space . . . It must have shown on my face, because she smiled. She knew she had me.

Dylan clocked it too; his one ally was wavering.

'This sucks,' he said, slithering further down in his chair. Mum switched her attention to him. She'd done her research, knew exactly how close the stinking shop was to the nearest skate park and comic bookstore.

As she talked, it all came crashing in on me. I wasn't that attached to the cosy semi we rented, but it was warm and comfortable. There was a stubbly-lawned garden to kick around in in summer, and it was three streets away from my friends. Now we'd be moving to the worst side of town, living in someone else's place – Leah Stoke's house. A place where tragedy hung in the air along with the dust.

I looked up and saw that Leah was looking back at me. Nobody but me heard her say: 'Come on, Ellie. You want to be a great artiste, and suffering is what makes people great.'

I stared at her, my mouth clamped shut. I couldn't really answer that one, could I? Suffering was what she did best. No wonder she didn't seem to mind.

The next few weeks involved packing, bickering, sulking and finally loading all our possessions into a shabby rented van and driving across town to our new prison – sorry, our new home.

The thing about David and Leah's neighbourhood is that you couldn't leave the back of a van open without someone to watch it. So, on moving day one of us had to be out on the street at all times. Mum, David, Dylan and I formed a silent chain – Mum passing things out of the van, the three of us ferrying them across the grimy, chewing gum-splattered expanse of pavement and through the shop to the flat upstairs. Leah was nowhere to be seen. I pictured her hiding in a tree or something, a wild animal startled by all the bustle.

My things – the things which mattered – only filled about five or six boxes. We'd moved around quite a lot since Mum and Dad had split up. Stuff had gone into storage and never come out. Bits had been accidentally shipped to Australia when Dad moved out there, or left behind by accident when we went from one place to another. Plus, I'd also had to give a lot of my possessions away before this move.

Because there are rules for dealing with Leah Stoke, just like there are rules for dealing with vampires. Laws that are bound in years of tradition and superstition until nobody in the Inner Circle would even think about breaching them. No loud noises. No sudden movements. You never mention the names Jane or Carey or ask for details of anything that happened on That Day. In fact, best not to push her for any information at all, which made conversation kind of difficult. These weren't unspoken rules – they were printed out on a leaflet by Mum's office at the charity and given out to members of the press before publicity events. There were a few extra ones for us as well – no violent movies, no first-person shooter games. No toy guns for Dylan, no gritty grime for me.

But the hardest rule of all was about what Mum and David liked to call Social Media, and what I called the basic human right to self-expression.

One ill-timed selfie at Thorpe Park was all it took to make the whole thing explode.

It was one of our first trips out as a proto-family. As if the best way of getting to know someone is by queuing together for two hours in the drizzle, followed by a three-minute drenching on a log flume. I thought I'd put in a pretty stellar performance, keeping the conversation going, dropping into my acclaimed Claudia Winkleman impression to liven up those awkward silences. At one point, I whipped out my phone and took a shot of Dylan and me, gurning stupidly. I whacked the resulting pic on Snapchat to show the world I was still alive. Little did I know that I had committed a heinous crime. Nay, an outrage, an unspeakable violation of Stoke Law. Because, unbeknownst to me, *Leah's left flipping eyebrow was in the picture.*

OK, it was more than an eyebrow. It was her whole profile and she was looking pretty dizzy and confused after an especially lethal roller coaster. I showed it to Mum, thinking she'd be pleased by this evidence of teen bonding, but instead her face went white and she looked a bit sick. She grabbed me by the shoulder and actually dragged me out of a queue we'd been in for ages. 'Take it off—'

'Down, Mum,' I corrected her.

'Whatever. Just get rid of it now, before someone in the press sees it.'

I was baffled – why would the world's press be looking at my Snapchat? (I bloody wish!) but Mum was freaking. She snatched my phone out of my hand and jabbed her fingers at random bits of the screen. Then David realised what was going on and started gabbling about privacy. He was straining to keep his tone reasonable while his voice pitched higher and higher, until it became a manic squeak.

'It's the media,' David explained in the frigid atmosphere of the car drive home, after his blood pressure had gone down. 'They twist things. They take the smallest little detail and make it into something big.'

So that's how I learned the final rule of living with the Stokes. Always protect Leah's privacy. No image of Leah may be taken and shared. No comment may be posted in reference to her. No letting anyone know where she might be, or whether she might be having fun. No tweets, no gifs, no buts.

I could have argued. I could have said that the charity had a Facebook page with over sixty thousand likes and posted pictures of Leah every time she made an especially tear-jerking speech. I could have mentioned her annual appearances at the Amazing Children Awards – a huge bash at a plush London hotel sponsored by a national newspaper, which had even been on telly once. I could have mentioned that time she met the Queen.

But how could I fight when they'd already suffered so much?

The thought of what happened to Leah, and to Jane and Carey, still made me want to cry. I tried to imagine what I would be like if I was her, if I'd seen what she'd seen when she was just seven years old. It was impossible to picture it – humans aren't built to understand pain like that. Your mind just blanks it out. When people talk about what Leah witnessed, they can't even bring themselves to say it. They just say she's 'the girl who . . . *you know* . . .'

David had every right to make special demands, to shelter her from harm. I'd just have to keep my online life all about me.

Perfect – that was just the way I liked it.

I did feel a nagging guilt though, as I climbed in the van to get the most important box from the back. It was sturdy, heavily taped up and ostentatiously marked EXTRA TAMPONS to stop Dylan getting nosy, but inside was a whole stack of notes, a ton of glitter, a top-of-the-range GoPro and a fold-up tripod that I'd bought with my summer job savings last year.

'This is a heavy one,' David commented mildly as I passed it into his arms. I avoided his eye and scuttled back into the van.

I didn't want to lie, but sometimes these things are necessary. I didn't mean any harm – I wasn't going to violate anyone's privacy, but still. If they found out that I was planning to run my own vlogging channel from my bedroom they'd probably explode with outrage. It would just have to stay secret for now.

'That's the lot,' Mum said, plonking down the last rickety box on the shop floor and pushing her hair out of her eyes with a grubby wrist.

The door closed behind her and, for a couple of moments, we were all still. A muted beam of sunlight poured in through the dirt-misted windows, lighting up millions of atoms of dust as they flew around us – the crumbled remains of dead books suspended in the air. I breathed in a big noseful of stale paper and damp, mingled with the kebab shop fumes from outside. My new home.

On the back of the door hung a faded but cheery sign, hand drawn in felt tip by a much younger Leah, which said *Back soon!* Just in case someone was desperate for a book whilst David was in the loo. The counter was tatty, most of the space on it was taken up by a CAREY collection box and a cash register covered in faded Post-it notes. Behind it was a glass case with allegedly valuable first editions inside, although they looked just as ratty as the other books to me.

Underneath the case, I caught sight of a green light blinking sluggishly through the murk – an ancient Wi-Fi router, encrusted with grime and half buried under a pile of junk mail. The slow-beating heart of my future multimedia empire.

The rest of the shop was a maze of shelves, narrow corridors, dead ends. David had told me once that he'd deliberately set it up not to make any sense at all.

'A good bookshop is like a voyage of discovery,' he liked to say. 'You find things quite by accident which might change your life.' I looked at some of the faded spines of the books on display: *Old Moore's Almanac*, *Lady Good-For-Nothing, a Novel* by 'Q' and a collection of *Fifty Shades of Grey* built into a little pyramid. David's amazing store of knowledge, I presumed.

Looming from the top of the cash desk was a narrow wooden staircase which led up to what David liked to call the 'mezzanine' – a crooked balcony crammed with even more bookshelves. It looked like the whole thing could drop on his head at any moment.

'Not many people go up there,' he admitted when he saw me staring. 'But they should, that's where I keep all the good stuff!'

'Um, maybe I'll check it out later,' I said, treading the line between politeness and dripping, venomous sarcasm. I bent down, grabbed EXTRA TAMPONS and started lugging it towards the chipped wooden door that hid the staircase to the flat. I wasn't going to stand still in this place for long.

It took several days to work out just how much the shop, and the crummy flat above it, completely and utterly sucked. It was even worse than I imagined.

For a start, it was draughty. I'd get up every morning and need to put on my unicorn slippers and fluffy dressing gown just to get as far as the bathroom. Once inside, I'd have to run the shower for at least ten minutes before the water got semi-warm, by which time I'd have everyone banging on the door to get in because there was ONLY ONE BATHROOM FOR FIVE PEOPLE.

Mum had filled every room with plug-ins and scent diffusers but, despite her efforts, the book smell was starting to cling to my stuff, and everything in the flat was cold. The plates in the kitchen cupboard chilled the food before we got it to the table, my laptop was like a block of ice on my knees. Even my clothes turned my skin to goose pimples when I slipped them on.

David didn't seem to feel it and had a nasty habit of wandering around wearing sleep-shorts and a T-shirt, displaying his hairy legs and bony bare feet to the world. Leah had this hideous brown fleece that she slipped into as soon as she came home, somehow managing to look elegantly sloppy. She didn't complain.

David and Mum spent most of their evenings in the family room. They played Scrabble, listened to Radio 4, read books and newspapers. What they didn't do was watch TV because David didn't have one. Weirdo.

'Books are so much better,' he had said the first time we met him. 'You use your imagination. When you watch TV it's all served up to you on a plate – you don't get to *think*.'

Thinking is overrated. After a hard day's thinking at school, the last thing I wanted to do was come home and think some more.

So, I spent most of the time in my room, listening to Dylan's muffled gaming next door, watching a few seconds of YouTube footage followed by a whole lot of buffering, and trying not to think about the fact that Leah had once slept here. Ten years ago, after Jane and Carey were gone, little Leah had all her nightmares in here, looking up at the heart-shaped crack in the ceiling and calling for a mum who was gone for ever. Shuddering, I closed the iPad case and went out to the landing to the so-called family room.

Mum, David and Leah were gathered there on the battered brown sofa. Leah was asleep, leaning against her dad's shoulder. His arm was around her, keeping her warm, and her honey hair spread across her shoulders, shining in the lamplight. Mum sat upright on the other side of him, reading a dog-eared Mills & Boon from the shop, her cup of tea resting on the pile of books they used as a side-table. She looked almost prim – except for the giant pig slippers.

'Ellie, hello!' she said as if she was surprised to see me. 'Why don't you come in and we'll play a game of cards.'

'The iPad's stopped working,' I said, sinking down onto a stack of encyclopaedias by the door. 'My phone's got no reception, and the internet's *sllllooooowwwww*.'

'I know.'

'Last night, Gloria texted me that her dad has won a holiday in Barbados and I didn't see it until seven this morning. Mum, she's my best friend, she thought I didn't care.'

'I know.'

David rested his hand on Mum's as if to say *I'm here for you, be strong when dealing with your hell-daughter.* Then Leah stirred in her sleep.

We all tensed up, and I felt hot suddenly – ashamed maybe, but also completely pissed off. I spun on my foot and walked away.

Late that night I lay in bed listening to all the weird sounds of the shop settling down for the night – the plink-plink of ancient hot-water pipes, the creak of floorboards. Through the tissue-thin walls, I heard Dylan muttering in his sleep and David's short, neat little snores drifted across the hall-way. Somewhere downstairs in the shop, an ancient book got tired of clinging onto life and fell to the floor with a papery slither.

I had got used to the pinkish glow that the kebab shop sign next door cast onto my ceiling. I told myself it was like being in an apartment in New York, with a sleazy neon sign blinking outside my window. But what I hated were the fights that sometimes started out there – I never knew whether someone was going to get seriously hurt; whether, because I didn't call the police, somebody would die.

I wondered if it was like this when Leah first lived here and, for a minute, I hated David. All this stuff he went on about, putting Leah first, doing what was right for her. How could this have been right for her? No wonder she didn't sleep in this room any more.

Which reminded me of the persistent, scratchy thought that had bothered me from the day we'd moved in. Leah now slept in a tiny box-room at the end of the corridor, but all that was in there was a neatly made single bed, a wardrobe, chair and desk stacked up with homework books. I'd never seen a less personalised girl's bedroom. I'd also never seen the light on in there, and never seen her come out of it in the morning.

Creeping softly into the corridor, I looked at Leah's bedroom door – it was slightly open, and no crack of light showed from inside. Curiosity pushed me forward. I wasn't thinking, had no plan, but just nudged the door open a tiny bit more.

An earth-shattering creak pierced the silence, but nobody was there to hear it.

Leah's bed was empty.

So, if this wasn't Leah's room – where did she sleep?

Chapter 2

Leah, present day

This time I am using a weapon and he doesn't notice until the baseball bat hits him on the back of the neck, followed up with a swift kick behind his knees, which makes him crumple and crash to the floor. As soon as he's down, it's the work of moments to kick him hard in the ribs and slam onto him, trapping him there. He doesn't make a sound, just a light sigh as the air rushes out of his lungs. His eyes are glazed over, he still doesn't know who I am. I punch him in the throat . . .

No. The leg kick means he's on his front, I can't punch him in the throat. Instead . . .

As he tries to lift his head, I slam it downwards and hear a crack as his jaw hits the floor. Then, while he's dazed, I get up and start kicking.

Closing my eyes, I can feel it, my steel toecaps slamming into his soft body. I wonder what damage I would cause; how many it would take before he curls into a whimpering ball. I wonder whether I'd be able to stop, and when. When I see blood? When he begs me? When he throws up? When he says sorry?

Why should I stop? He didn't.

Well, not until he got to me.

The thought bubbles up in my head, breaking my concentration, and letting a crack of light in. I feel Dad's hand squeezing my arm gently.

'Are you ready, Leah?' And then he says the same thing he always says: 'You know you don't have to do this if you don't want to.'

I smile, shaking off the mental image of the groaning, broken man and focusing on reality. I open my eyes to the sunlight of the room I'm really in. I take in the big, draughty windows, tired parquet floor and the faded tissue-paper collages that decorate the walls. It's either a church hall or a community centre, I didn't really listen when they told me, but fortunately it's written on the palm of my hand, in case I forget. It takes me a couple of seconds to adjust but that's OK, people don't expect what I'm about to do to come easily. My splintered wooden chair scrapes as I stand up and a sense of calm settles on me. I slowly climb the steps to the podium where I can look down on them all. I see grave, pink faces – women over fifty who have dressed smartly for this occasion, with their bags held on their laps, some with a tissue already twisted between their fingers. They are organised women and they have come prepared to cry.

Time to do my job. I step forward to the lectern, take a deep breath and engage autopilot.

'Thank you once again to the wonderful people at' – *check hand* – 'St Mary's Church Hall, for providing us with such a lovely space and a delicious lunch, and for all your incredible hard work raising money for CAREY. I won't take up too much of your time, but I wanted to share what I've learned with you. I want to talk, not about crime or violence, but about the power of forgiveness . . .'

Forgiveness. As if I could tell them what that is.

Over the years I've learned the right way to think about it. How pointless it is to cling to hatred and anger when all you're doing is hurting yourself. How learning to forgive is about setting yourself free from all that negativity. I've talked about it with priests, knights of the realm, reality TV stars and housewives – all prating the same, tired old lines churned out by Facebook memes. But it's one thing to know in your head what's true and good and right, and another to feel it.

And so the only way I can use the word forgiveness without feeling sick is to picture him, lying on the floor, shaking under my boot and to promise myself I don't really mean it.

We get McDonald's on the way home, the way we used to when I was little. These days the plain hamburger disappears in two bites and there's no plastic Happy Meal toy, but at least it means I don't have to sit around the dinner table with Claire, Ellie and Dylan tonight.

They're too much, all of them. Dylan runs everywhere – I can hear his footsteps, *clumpclumpclump*, knocking over books and ornaments as he pelts along. Ellie plunges down onto the sofa, kicks off her overpriced shoes and just leaves them there to pile up, just like the trail of toys, half-eaten sweets and half-finished drawings Carey used to leave behind everywhere she went. And she talks – oh, she never stops talking. You could never imagine we were almost the same age, give or take six months or so. Since she moved in, bits of glitter have got into everything – the bathroom drain, the hall carpet – there was even a bit floating in my breakfast cereal yesterday. What is this thing with glitter? She throws it over people, apparently. I can't think of anything more annoying.

Claire means well. She doesn't think she has changed much around the house at all, but she seems to be obsessed with air fresheners. The flat is full of oils, diffusers and plug-ins and the air is thick with sticky, cloying scents, which means home doesn't smell like home any more. Every room has a small device plugged into it, spraying out puffs of artificial atmosphere into the house – Winter Spice, Summer Glen, Happy Family. Every load of washing is doused in gallons of fabric conditioner so even my clothes smell weird.

And she has moved my chair.

There used to be a chair by the kitchen door. It was old – even when I was little, it was old, a 1970s relic inherited from Grandma. It had a padded plastic seat and it was never very comfortable. As a kid, I'd sit on it at breakfast time, kneeling so that my chin reached over the top of the table. If I was wearing shorts or a skirt, my legs would always stick to the cushion and I'd try to keep as still as possible, knowing that as soon as I moved, it would rip at my skin and sting like hell.

I haven't sat on that chair for years – the seat was all torn and nasty bits of foam were sticking out of it – but since we moved to the shop it has always stood by the kitchen door, underneath the landline, just in case anyone wanted to sit down when they were on the phone.

And now, it's gone.

'It was a bit bashed up,' Claire says. 'And we needed extra space for the bigger breakfast table. We're picking it up from IKEA tomorrow, want to come?'

'But it's always been there,' I say, knowing how weak it sounds.

'Love, we've put it outside for the council to collect,' Dad says. 'Do you want me to go and get it back in? It's only rained a little, the cushion will soon dry out . . .' I see Claire's shoulders tense up, but she doesn't say anything. She's picking her battles.

'No, no.' I shake my head. I know I'm just being silly – it's only a chair, there are bigger things to lose. Everything must change.

I wonder how much things have changed for him after ten years. The friends he had when he went in have probably all drifted away. His mum died – I know that because I read it in the papers. They printed pictures of a sad, thin woman who looked like she was trying to shrink away to nothing, mouth pressed shut and eyes downcast against the hate which flew at her. I doubt anyone calls him Crow any more – nobody but the press and our publicity leaflets.

Maybe prison has turned him into a broken-down wreck, full of regret at what he did, but I think it will have made him harder. Whatever crap he spun to the Parole Board is all lies – he'll be leaner and tougher, and still ready with his knife. I know him better than them, and I can feel the truth of it.

That won't bother me, though, as he won't see me until it's too late.

I take out my pocketknife, small and sharp, and make my way downstairs, out of the back door, to the alley where the bins are kept. It stinks of piss and my footsteps are cushioned by crushed cans and old crisp packets, as I pick my way over to the chair. It really is a ramshackle piece of furniture – nails sticking out of it, varnish all worn off – but its tacky blue gingham pattern makes me smile. The knife slides easily into the cushion, and the plastic makes a satisfying sound as it gives way under the blade. I cut a perfect square of chair-skin and curl it between my fingers – then I fold it into my pocket and go back inside.

I read in a newspaper once – one of the thoughtful, more considerate newspapers that didn't call for his hanging – that he learned to read in prison, that he entered a special education programme and got his GCSE in English. A testament, said the article, 'to the concept of prison as a means of rehabilitation and reconciliation, rather than the revenge of the aggrieved party upon the criminal'. I tried to picture it, to imagine him curled up in that narrow bunk with a copy of *The Three Musketeers*, reading the same words I did, being transported to the same places, loving the same people.

After it happened, I read that book until my eyes ached, poring over the kitchen table hour after hour, letting the words wash over me and helping me forget who I was. I'd kneel there until my legs went numb, being d'Artagnan instead of me. When I finally had to move because of hunger, call of nature or fading daylight, I'd rip my bare legs off the plastic cushion on the chair and the pain would remind me I was real.

I was sitting there, around six months after that day, when Dad came in.

'Petal, can I have a word?'

I can't remember what I replied. My memory is patchy like that. I probably told him not to call me Petal. I was expecting another trip to see Tina, who Dad called the Shrink Lady when he thought I couldn't hear. I'd have to endure another few hours of staring at her crocheted waistcoat and trying not to answer any of her questions, in case they made me feel something. I slid low on the chair, my legs squeaking against the cushion, and met Dad's eye. I didn't want him to butter me up with Petal.

'I've been thinking very hard lately about where we live, my job and how I want to make a difference in the world . . . and spend more time with you, of course,' he said. 'We've got some money coming. If we sell this house, you and me, we can buy a new place. Start afresh. What do you say?'

He didn't explain it all back then. I probably wouldn't have understood this need he had, to make sense of what had happened and turn it into something good. I've heard the talk since at countless fundraisers – the idea of going into troubled communities, sharing books with them, how education is an escape route from crime. But even at that age, I still understood that he wasn't really giving me a choice. I was a small, drifting thing who couldn't change anything, especially not my father's mind.

I must have nodded because he cuddled me and called me his brave girl.

It happened slowly – nothing changed for a while as Dad sold the house and set things up. My life trickled along, until I'd convinced myself it wouldn't happen at all. I watched the boxes being packed, I played with the bubble wrap, and helped fold each of our yellow dinner plates into old pages of newspaper, but it felt like a game.

I messed about. I hid things. I used my felt tip pens to make brightly coloured little signs for the three piles: *Keep, Chuck, Charity shop.*

Outside in the garden, Dad had started a bonfire – old bits of worktop, empty shoeboxes – nothing sentimental. But when someone is gone, everything's sentimental, even the old Boden catalogues they didn't really like. Dad was staring into the fire, his eyes glassy and his cheeks wet. I slipped my hand into his as I knew this would make him stop crying, and for a while we watched the flames eating through wood and cardboard, flaring and darting, leaving everything they touched coated in black. Then I noticed a scrap of soft grey fuzz in his other hand.

'Is that Kentucky?' I asked.

Dad jumped guiltily. 'I just found him, love. I know you don't like him any more.'

I snatched my hand out of Dad's and pulled Kentucky away from his grasp. But I couldn't stand to hold him, either. I dropped him onto the damp grass between us, like he was already on fire. His big teddy bear head lolled forward, black nose snuffling at the dandelion leaves, beady eyes looking blankly down. I couldn't believe that I once thought those eyes were alive.

'YOU WERE GOING TO BURN KENTUCKY!' I shouted. 'That's HORRIBLE.'

I ran inside, away from him, and away from the slouched grey shape on the lawn, inside to where Uncle Jeff, who was helping with the move, was sorting through our furniture.

'This old chair can go.' He held the old plastic-cushioned chair by its back, hovering over the *Chuck* pile. 'What do you reckon?'

A cold sticky feeling crept over my body. My heart was beating hard and I could hear Dad coming up the garden path, back to hug me and soothe me and trap me. I screamed, 'NO', louder than I ever had before, and ran upstairs, slamming myself into the semi-packed room I used to share with Carey.

I needed someone. But Kentucky was gone, he had never even existed. And my friends at school were just blurs now, flimsy cartoon characters who had never seen anyone die, and cared about unicorns and sparkly charm bracelets. I needed my mum, but she was far away too: with the stars, with the angels, up in heaven – so many ways to explain to a child what dead means.

All I knew was that when I closed my eyes, there were no stars or angels. I saw a knife, my strange friend with the waggly eyebrows, and blood.

Chapter 3

Ellie

If you had tortured me, I would have denied it, but in truth I'd thought a lot about what I was going to wear to the gig that evening. My skirt, my sneakers, my jangling accessories had all been carefully chosen to look cool and relaxed, but with a few extra touches so I didn't just look the same as everyone else. Tucked in my coat pocket were two little plastic containers of glitter to chuck over everyone later, and an apple.

Mum had been quiet throughout the drive to the venue. One advantage of living in such a crappy area was that MumCabs Ltd was fully operational and driving lessons would be paid for as soon as my provisional licence came through. But normally when she drove me to parties, she chatted all the way there, usually about the ones she'd been to as a kid or asking me excruciating questions about what 'they're all wearing these days'. Not this time. As we drove, the streetlights flashed yellow light on my chilly legs, and she spoke.

'That skirt – um, it's pretty short.'

'Oh no.' I could not believe this was happening. 'We are not having this conversation,' I said.

'What conversation?'

'The "you're not going out wearing that" conversation.'

That's the kind of talk other girls have with their mothers, it's not us. As far as I was concerned, we had a deal – she never went off on one about 'that's not a skirt it's a belt,' and I never went out dressed like a stripper. We'd never actually spoken about it, but that was how it worked. Still Mum pressed on, telling me she had a right to be worried about safety, that working for CAREY really makes you think . . .

'Oh, come on, Mum. It's not CAREY, it's bloody Dave, isn't it?'

'Ellie! . . . And it's *David*, Ellie.'

I stared ahead. Mum had been Super Safety woman ever since she'd started working for the Campaign Against Reoffending and for Empowering Youth two years before. Dylan and I had to have our phones with us all the time, tell her where we were going, never talk to strangers, yada yada, but this was new, this was David. I'd seen the judgey look he and Leah had exchanged when I swept past them on my way out, and I could just imagine him grabbing Mum and suggesting she had a word.

She was the one who'd moved us into a second-hand bookshop in the middle of a war zone, the whole point of which was to encourage local criminals inside, in the hope they'll stop mugging people and start reading Dickens instead. Neither of them had the right to lecture me on safety.

We both kept stubbornly quiet until we pulled up at the end of the street where the venue was.

'Got your phone and your purse?'

I nodded.

'Got loads of glitter to annoy everyone with?' she asked.

I let myself smile a little bit and nodded.

'Got your apple, for some unknown reason?'

I smiled a bit more and took it out of my pocket, then gave it a polish on my controversial skirt. The apple was juicy-looking and pinkish red on one side.

She shook her head and laughed softly as I got out. I suppressed a low chuckle as I walked away. It just proved to me that the apple was working.

The band was still setting up when I walked in, but the place was already pretty full. It was a good turnout because the first support act, a moronic un-woke outfit called Bitches Tell Lies, went to our school. A knot of girls had gathered at the front to try and grab the attention of the bass guitarist, aka The Vaguely Good Looking One. At school I'd say he was about a six or seven, but on stage with a guitar everyone morphs into a nine point five. A ten if you sing too. The lads had taken up position around the bar, trying to outdrink each other. One couple was sucking face, although it was a tad early in the evening for that.

Nobody was eating an apple, except me.

I let my teeth crunch into it as I walked across the room.

'Nice apple, can I have a bite?'

'Get lost, Jason.' I said it with a smile, though, because Jason was quite nice.

'What's with the apple?' one girl asked.

'Just making sure I get my five-a-day,' I said brightly. All around me, people were looking at the apple, listening to me crunching on it. And I was pretending not to notice. I was just walking through a bar, eating an apple. That sort of thing happens every day.

Of course, the apple didn't work on Billie and Gloria, they knew my weirdness too well.

'Got to be different, haven't you?' Gloria rolled her eyes.

'What do you mean?' I protested. 'I was just hungry.'

First rule of doing something deliberately to get attention: never admit to it – you ruin the whole effect, and it sounds kind of pathetic when you explain it.

'Seriously though, hon, you look fucking amazing.' Gloria loves to say 'fuck'.

'Yeah, I would *literally* let you murder me right now,' Billie added. She likes exaggerating.

I was still brushing off these very welcome compliments when I saw him walking towards us – tall, with cropped hair and an easy smile that nearly made me drop my apple. Imagine violin music, slow motion and a soft focus on the meltiest brown eyes you've ever seen.

'Gloria, you moron, you forgot your phone,' the vision said. 'Dad made me come all the way back with it.' He lobbed the phone at his stepsister then turned on his trainers to leave, but I grabbed his jacket.

'Keiran, so glad I've run into you,' I said. 'I've got a job for you.'

Billie and Gloria laughed and went 'Oooooooh!' All my apple-induced cool was slipping away from me.

'Shut up, you two. It's a mural. I've just moved into ...
somewhere new ... and my room needs a mural to – well, to
take away the general crappiness of it.'

Keiran ran his hand over his chin thoughtfully, callused
fingertips scraping against stubble. There was a splash of
magenta paint on his thumbnail. Yes, not pink – magenta. 'I
never did an inside painting before,' he said. 'Could do it but
would need to see the space. I'd just do my usual stuff, yeah?'

'Yeah,' I said. 'Just no gothic stuff or anything though. I'm
not soft but it's house rules.' Besides, I wanted this mural to
be a celebration, the start of something new – not the sort of
thing you announce with skulls.

He nodded, and then he was gone, leaving me to Gloria
and Billie chanting, 'Keiran, I've got a job for you. It's a
REALLY BIG JOB ... Come up to my ROOM, Keiran!'

'He's a street artist. I like street art,' I said. 'Besides, my
room needs tarting up – it's not exactly on DBLG brand at the
moment.'

'So, tell me, how's it going at home?' Billie asked, switching
the subject before things got awkward with Gloria. 'Can't be
easy living with the girl who ... you know ...'

'She's, well ...' they leaned forward, eager for snippets of
information about life with the Inspiring One. 'Actually, I
don't want to talk about it. Vlog meeting first.'

We commandeered a booth at the back of the venue and
talked ideas. We'd only been going a few months but we'd
done loads of posts and had gained a few hundred subscribers. I was the one who'd started the whole thing – the 'little

girl' of *Dream Big Little Girl* was me, so technically it was my channel. But it's more fun to do it with other people, so Gloria handled the beauty, and Billie did the music. I did the stupid stuff that pulled it all together. I wrote silly skits and sketches and threw glitter – a *lot*. People tended to give me a wide berth on nights out as I was always packing a pot or two.

Glitter and comedy, that's what made us different. We messed about. We thought it was hilarious; we just had to get more subscribers who agreed.

I quickly told them my latest genius idea, which involved reproducing the end bit of *Dirty Dancing*.

'People will expect the lift,' Billie said, waving her hand dismissively. 'And none of us are exactly . . .' Billie sighed, looking down at her curvy figure. It was a perfectly nice figure, but we knew there was no point telling her that.

'My stepdad could bring a forklift home from work,' Gloria suggested.

There was something about the way Gloria said 'forklift' that made us all burst into laughter. And then, the evening just became brilliant.

'It was, like, *hilarious*,' I told Mum as we got back home. 'We kept shouting "Forklift!" then lifting each other up in the mosh pit, until people were watching us instead of the band. Then I threw glitter all over Leroy and Kate, and Leroy went mad. Then everyone else started shouting FORKLIFT! without really knowing why they were doing it, and then—'

'Shh, Ellie – it's one a.m.,' Mum said, her voice scratchy with tiredness. We were inside the shop now. The light switch by the door didn't work, so Mum had her phone torch on, casting eerie shadows around the stacks and shelves.

'FORKLIFT!' I shouted, just to lighten the mood. The books absorbed the sound, cushioning the air around me with leathery pages, but it didn't stop Mum snapping at me to shut up and asking what I'd been drinking. All the fun of the evening drained away. I was here again.

The weekend went downhill from then on. Next morning, Mum hustled me into the car, along with Dylan and Leah. 'I thought it would be fun to choose my wedding dress together,' she said.

It must have been a long time since Mum had had any proper fun.

The shop was called Bridal Dreams. Billie, Gloria and I used to walk past it on the way to school. We always thought Bridal Screams was a better name for it, and it hadn't got any more cheerful looking since then. Five shiny white mannequins filled the window, arranged in awkward poses, smooth white elbows jutting out at weird angles like parents dancing in a nightclub.

They wore blank expressions and huge, huge dresses – so much lace and frill and taffeta that there was barely room for anything else in the window. But in the far corner, so tucked away that you would hardly notice him, stood a neglected-looking male dummy in a high-pointed shirt collar, cream-coloured cravat and matching waistcoat. A sheen of dust had collected like dandruff on the shoulders of his dark grey tailcoat.

'One groom, five brides,' I said as we stood outside. 'Is that even legal?'

Mum rolled her eyes, Dylan wasn't even listening, but I noticed the corner of Leah's mouth twitch as we pressed the bell to go in.

Yes, the bell. This wasn't one of your ordinary shops open to any old riffraff off the street. Oh no, you had to ring them in advance and make an appointment.

The shop was all cream and gold, like being inside a wedding cake. Everywhere I looked was bright and clean and adorned with little cherubs.

'Welcome, hello!' A middle-aged lady with a pencil skirt and her hair in a bun was rushing towards us. 'I'm Anya. How lovely to see you, and congratulations of course.' She spoke in hushed tones, like she was in church, or in a doctor's surgery about to break bad news about Those Test Results. She looked at Leah and her mouth gaped. 'Oh! Oh, well we'll have no trouble finding you the dress of your dreams.'

Mum shifted awkwardly, clutching her bag to her chest. 'Actually, it's me.'

Anya looked suitably agonised. Good. Mum spoke again quickly to cut off any more apologies.

'I'm looking for something romantic but not too showy,' she said. 'It's a second marriage. And the groom isn't into smart.'

Anya smiled a sympathetic smile that said: *Men*. She looked Mum up and down and her brow wrinkled a bit. 'I'm sure we'll find the perfect dress for you. But I will have to warn you, we only have sample sizes in store – once you order, we can provide the right size. Now if you could all just slip off your shoes?' She frowned down at my grubby Vans. I shuffled them off and stepped barefoot onto the cream, fuzzy carpet. Mum and Leah did likewise. As Dylan slipped out of his, I pretended to be choked by his awful foot odour. She then handed us each a pair of white gloves.

'Some of the dresses are very delicate,' she explained. 'This stops them smudging.'

Dylan's straight male instincts had already compelled him to flop down on a fancy chair in the corner with his phone and bury himself in Zombies Versus Babies. Anya led Mum towards the 'mature second marriage, nothing too fancy' department in the back room of the shop, leaving Leah and me flicking through the dresses on the rails.

'Hideous ... hideous ... gross ...' I dismissed each one. 'They all look the same. Why does everybody want to look the same?'

Leah just shrugged and I wished Billie was here instead.

'OK, if you had to, which one would you pick?' I asked.

Leah dropped the cream satin skirt she'd been holding like it had given her an electric shock. 'Me?'

'Yes, supposing the love of your life wanted to get married but only if you picked a dress from this shop. Which one?'

'I don't know, they're all so pretty.'

'No, they're not.'

'No,' she echoed. 'They're not. I think I'd rather get married in my underwear.'

'I think I'd pick the grossest one, as a true test of my man's love.' I ran over to a mannequin dressed in a ruffled number that looked like it had been made out of used, screwed-up tissues. 'If he'd marry me wearing this, he'd definitely be crazy about me.'

Was that . . . could that have been a laugh?

We wandered off in different directions, and I tried on some long gloves and struck a pose in the gigantic gilt mirror near the fitting rooms. And then it happened.

I swear that I saw what I saw, even though afterwards I could hardly believe it myself. I never even told Billie or Gloria because I thought they wouldn't believe me.

In the mirror, I saw Leah crouch down and take something out of her pocket. Something shiny and metallic. It looked like . . . it couldn't be . . . was that a *knife*?

It was. Small and sharp, I couldn't tell if it was a penknife or a flick knife, but it looked wickedly pointed. I froze, fixing a false grin on my face in case she looked up. She used the blade to slice into the fabric, cutting from the bottom of one of the ruffles where a tear wouldn't be seen. The blade must have been incredibly sharp, the satin gave way under it, until she had a small square in her hand. I saw her fingers stroke the fabric gently. Then she folded the knife up, tucked both things into her pocket and pretended to tie her shoelace.

Knives were definitely against the Rules. She should never want to see a knife again, and yet she'd used it so neatly and confidently . . . I shuddered.

Act natural, I told myself. So I worked on some glove selfies until a few moments later Anya appeared beside me, glaring disapprovingly and announcing, 'Your Mother Is Ready.'

Mum stepped forward in a simple cream sheath-dress that hung softly from delicate shoulder straps. Still shocked from what I'd just seen, the sight of her made me catch my breath.

'What do you think?' She had a nervous smile and fidgeted with the straps.

She looked like Mum, only more special – stronger and softer at the same time. I struggled to find the right thing to say, to make her happy without feeling corny or lame. Why is it so hard to tell your mother she looks beautiful?

'You look really lovely, Claire,' Leah said, smiling and giving Mum a loose hug. I followed her, feeling lame and second-rate.

Dylan looked up from his game, checked out the sight of his mother in the most amazing, expensive dress she'd ever worn, found nothing of interest and looked back down again.

'Now for you girls,' Mum said.

Ah, the moment I'd been dreading – Leah and I, side by side in matching bridesmaid outfits. The tall willowy blonde and the short, curly-haired brunette with a Pringles addiction. What a dream team.

Anya tipped her head to one side and pressed her forefinger to her lip as she thought. 'Hmm ... to suit both skin tones ... what about lilac?'

Within ten minutes I was bundled into a changing room and trussed up in a rustly mauve, satin A-line number with a flouncy petticoat underneath.

'Come on, love,' Mum said, working the zip up my back, link by link. 'Breathe in, just a little. We'll get one that fits properly later on, this is just to get an idea of what it'll look like.'

The curtain from the cubicle next to me rattled aside. I heard Anya give a tiny gasp, a sob of emotion.

'After all you've been through, I hope you get to wear something like this someday,' she whispered.

I stuck my head through the heavy brocade curtains.

Leah was standing in front of a large, three-sided mirror, reflected back at us from triple angles. Her hair was scooped up from her neck and gathered loosely in a clip on the back of her head, her lightly tanned shoulders sloped into the most beautiful bridal dress I had ever seen. The silk seemed to flow down her, moving and catching the light as she turned, the boned corset flattered her tiny waist. Something about the dreamy, serene expression on her face made me feel uneasy. I thought about the knife and the small, precise cuts she'd made, and I shivered. She turned and looked at us, calm and perfect, and met my eye. *Was she enjoying this?*

'Actually,' she said to me, 'I think I'd get married in this one.'

Chapter 4

Leah

Dad makes a soft scratching sound on the bookcase that serves as my door.

'Leah, are you home?'

I hesitate for a moment. I don't want to talk to him, not until I have made sense of the afternoon and the strange feelings it has triggered. But I also know that if I stay quiet, that will plant seeds in Dad's mind, seeds of worry that will take root in his head, until he realises what a mad daughter he has. I don't want that to happen yet, not before I've done what I need to do.

'I'm here.'

Dad never comes into my hiding place; he knows not to. I unfold myself from the mattress on the floor and slip out to meet him. We sit together on piles of old *History Today*, looking down at the shop.

'I hear you've been trying on wedding dresses,' he says.

'I didn't realise the shop woman recognised me,' I said. 'I hope Claire's not too upset.'

Dad's eyebrows flicker upwards in mild surprise. 'Of course not. Why would she be? Anyway, I wanted to show you something.'

He takes me by the hand. He likes to do that, and I curl my fingers around his to show him that I'm OK.

He leads me down the wooden mezzanine steps – I can see the *Back soon!* sign hanging on the shop door. Keeping my hand in his, he leads me to the tiny room at the rear of the shop which we use for storage. There he lets my hand drop gently, and clambers over the boxes and bags, moving them back and forth like a complex Jenga-type puzzle, muttering non-swearwords under his breath as he goes – *oh fluffing heck where did I put it?* Finally, he reaches some old battered ones crammed right into a corner. I stand patiently while he struggles back towards me.

He is carrying a cardboard box wrapped in a black bin liner and wound around with tape. It's dusty, untouched for years, but Dad takes a pair of scissors and cuts the tape, pulling the semi-rotten plastic aside. It comes away in little black tatters, scattering itself like dark snow on the lids of other boxes.

He opens the lid and there it is, a nest of ivory lace and satin, a twiggy garland of peach and cream silk flowers laid on top. The texture of the dress looks brittle and slightly crunchy; it has clearly been in this box for many years.

'It's your mother's dress,' Dad says. He moves the garland carefully aside, as if it's something holy, and takes the dress by the shoulders, lifting it up. The stiff bodice flaps out, the petticoats bulk under the skirt, and for a moment it is almost like Mum's body is filling the dress. I almost expect a white hand to push itself out of the lace, leg-of-mutton sleeve. A memory flashes through my head – throwing my arms around

41

narrow hips, feeling the warmth against the side of my face, hearing a rumbling tummy while a hand strokes my hair. That's who she is to me now.

'I'm sorry,' Dad says. 'Did I upset you?'

I shake my head quickly.

'I wanted to show it to you, to tell you that it's yours now. For when you get married one day.'

For a second I wonder if I have heard him right. Then I do what's required of me. I hug him and say thank you, and quietly resign myself to the fact I'll never get to wear a simple, flowing gown like the one I tried on today, that I would never have to go dress shopping and choose one for myself. This haunted dress is all I will need.

Many things about my future have been decided for me. It is for the best. Why study far away, when I could stay at home and attend our local university? Forget about a degree in criminology, it wouldn't be good for me. English Literature is perfect, haven't I always loved books? Then maybe a teaching qualification, or something in media so I can bring my new skills back to the charity afterwards. Now it seems my wedding is mapped out too – although Dad would have trouble finding anyone prepared to marry a freaky bag of issues like me.

And I should feel grateful – being a freaky bag of issues is a small price to pay for being alive.

Oh yes, did I mention how lucky I am?

When I was small, I saw an old film called *Pollyanna* and for a while Mum and Dad had encouraged me to play the

Glad Game she'd created. *I'm glad I have to go to school because girls in some countries don't get to. I'm glad it's spinach for dinner, because that means I'll grow up healthy and strong.* The whole thing struck me as a complete, global adult-induced con to control children and stop them moaning about eating their greens.

But then afterwards, after it happened, the Glad Game changed.

That night I sat in a cubicle at the hospital for hours, a pale blue NHS blanket heavy on my shoulders, policemen hovering around, waiting and wondering if I was going to say anything useful. Dad was by my side but silent, in shock. Every now and then he would look at me and open his mouth to speak but no words came, and I was thankful for it. I never wanted to speak again in case my words killed someone else. At some point, someone had given me a box of juice and I held it, unopened, in my hand, running my fingers back and forth over the plastic straw while my mouth grew drier.

Through the curtain, I overheard a nurse talking to one of the officers. 'She's a lucky one, that kid. Thank God, not a scratch on her.'

At the time I didn't fully understand what had happened, but I remembered her words. I was lucky. Did that mean Mummy was OK? Did that mean my horrible little sister would burst in any minute to steal my juice and grab all the attention?

Later, I read it in the newspapers – *Lucky Leah*. I remember seeing a quote from Dad once: 'I'm grateful that I have my beautiful daughter.' It even says it on the CAREY leaflets: *thankfully, Leah survived the attack.*

Volunteers said it all the time in one form or another, usually by accident in some clumsy attempt to cheer Dad up. Crass variations on *at least you've still got one left.* One devout and very intense volunteer called Joy even mentioned it to me.

It was in my early teens. Joy was looking after me while Dad had a meeting and we were sitting in the CAREY office, silent except for the clack and slide of Joy's thin grey knitting needles. She was making a shapeless brown thing out of straggly, itchy wool. Whatever it was I hoped it wasn't for me.

'Do you ever think about why?' she asked, without even looking up.

I knew what she was talking about straight away. It was the question I expected everyone to ask, but nobody had ever asked it – not Dad, not the police (well, not outright) and not even the handful of journalists Dad had let me speak to. I wondered why – were they afraid of the answer? Or did they just assume I didn't know?

Why had I survived, when the others hadn't? Why had the killer run off and left me alone?

I should have had a pat answer prepared but I didn't. Instead I was left gaping, squirming in my chair, feigning stupidity as Joy shifted her knitting around and began another row.

'You'll know one day,' she said. 'Everything happens for a reason. For now, rejoice and be glad that you are part of a bigger plan.'

*   *   *

So now the Glad Game is real. I am lucky. I am thankful. I'm glad it's raining today as at least I am here to see it. I'm glad I have Dad even though sometimes he loves me a little too much. I am glad that two noisy teenage brats have moved into my house because at least Claire and Dad will be happy. That cow Pollyanna was right – life is full of reasons to be cheerful.

I am trying not to think of *him*. He was lucky too. Lucky that Dad could find it in his heart to forgive. Lucky that he got clean, and that prison has done all those great things for him. And he's lucky that, for the moment at least, I cannot get to him.

That little square of satin from the wedding shop stays in my pocket for the next week, a fraying souvenir I had taken on impulse – a sudden need to destroy something. I stroke the soft fabric with my fingers as I wait for the bus or walk home from my Thursday class, and I think about the sensation of the smooth silky wedding dress fabric against my skin.

I realise something: I want to be able to choose. I want something for myself.

There's a shop, Proms And Beyond, on my route home that I never really noticed before. Now I find myself rooted to the paving slabs outside the door. I should be getting back – I mustn't worry Dad – but instead I find myself pushing the door and walking inside.

An electronic beeper goes off and the salesgirl looks up. I cringe but thankfully she goes straight back to her phone, a waterfall of blue hair tumbling down the side of her face, protecting both our private worlds. I glance at myself in the long mirror next to the changing room – my face is red and shiny from MMA, my hair still damp from the shower. No chance of being recognised. Plus the salesgirl is too young to be into that sort of thing anyway. Fifty-something women are my main fan base.

I spend a few moments flicking through the rows of clothes like they're the pages of a book, feeling the texture of each dress as I go. There's something relaxing, almost hypnotic about it, and I begin to see what people mean by retail therapy. Bright pink . . . no . . . baby blue . . . no . . . but what about . . .

This one.

It's black, with a deep sheen to the fabric. It doesn't look like much on the hanger and the flickering fluorescent light above isn't doing it any favours, but the material just feels so good. I run to the changing room (the salesgirl looks up, nods, then goes back to her phone) where I strip down to underpants and slip it over my head. For a few moments, I struggle with the halter-fastening at the nape of my neck but then, I'm in.

Oh. This is different. *I* am different.

The heavy fabric skims my hips and falls softly to the floor at just the right length. I turn and look over my shoulder like some stupid flirty Z-lister on the red carpet, my hair brushes my bare back and it feels wonderful and strange.

I love it. An instant, yearning love that I've never felt for an item of clothing before.

Ellie would like it, I think, and then I shake the thought away. Since when did I care about Ellie's opinions? I am not buying it to impress that vapid airhead.

No, there is a very sensible reason to purchase this dress: the Amazing Children Awards is coming up in a couple of months' time, and there's no way I can wear that bridesmaid's dress from Cousin Amber's wedding for the third time running.

I rush to the cashpoint. Dad wouldn't question the withdrawal, he's pretty relaxed about money, mainly because I don't need much of it – but he checks our debit card statements and I don't want him to see that I've spent three figures on clothes. On one dress.

Back home I hide it underneath Mum's old wedding dress in the storeroom, heart fluttering, a little bit scared of what I've done. Because now I've bought it I'm committed. Someday I'll have to wear it out into the light and give the world a glimpse of who I really am.

I just hope the world is ready.

Chapter 5

Boyd, before

The park is shit but it's better than home, where Troy can find me more easily. Of all the others, Troy is the one I hate most, my friend who is not my friend. The one who knows what to say to make me do what he wants, the one who says *go on, do it*, when he should be saying *ease off, mate*. I am Troy's bitch – all the others know it.

It was Troy who agreed for us to pick up the drugs at Bede Primary. He thought it was funny, watching all the kids toddle in and out with their Spiderman lunch boxes and Paw Patrol raincoats, kissing their smug mummies goodbye. All the while Jackson's little bro dashed through them, his little arms held out like an aeroplane and a massive flashy grin on his face, the way kids do when they're running. You couldn't tell there was that compartment cut out of the back of his puffa jacket, and little bruv was good at keeping secrets. He'd shrug out of his coat, undo the stuff taped inside and pass it through the fence to me as soon as the coast was clear.

'Epic,' Troy would say, laughing. And for a moment I felt a shred of his confidence settle on me. I stood up a bit straighter, reminding myself that I was part of the Crew, a king of the streets. Nobody would mess with me.

'Besides,' Troy said, his voice oozing like slime. 'That kid's got more balls than you'll ever have.'

Like I say, I hate Troy.

And because I hate Troy, I'm alone in the park like a loser.

I crack open a can of K cider and settle back on the stubbly grass, wondering if I could get away with a puff out here. But I'm too close to the kids' playground – it's the sunniest spot in the park and I don't want to move. So even though I really fancy one, I shrug the feeling off and try to enjoy the sunshine.

Enjoy the sunshine. Sort of thing my Nana used to say back before everything went to shit.

I'm watching her before I even know it. A girl I've never seen before, about six or seven I suppose. There's something very organised and grown-up about the way she sets the plastic picnic basket down on a patch of grass inside the kids' playground. Reaching inside, she shakes out a small red and white chequered tablecloth like Mary fucking Poppins and lays it down, making sure all four corners are folded out straight. I can hear her humming 'The Teddy Bears' Picnic'.

Two little plastic plates and cups are laid out: one for her, one for the greyish-brown teddy bear sat next to her, sagging back against her My Little Pony rucksack. *Wasn't she a bit old for teddies? I swear Kyle stopped playing with his soft toys when he was about three.*

Then she reaches into the picnic basket and pulls out this gigantic cupcake thing, sticks a birthday candle in.

You've got to be fucking kidding me.

I'm standing right next to her now. Didn't even feel myself get up and go over. I'm just there, staring at her. She's chatting away to the cuddly toy, leaving little gaps in her chat for the bear to answer. I can't hear any replies, but I'm not the right person to judge someone for hearing things that other people can't.

I sit down on the grass next to the picnic – it's wetter here and the damp seeps into my joggers – and look directly at the teddy bear.

'All right, mate?' I say.

She laughs and I feel this burst in my chest, like I've just levelled up in a game and the screen is covered in sparkly stars. *Achievement unlocked.*

It's like being with Kyle again. I forgot how simple it is with kids – you just talk. You don't have to worry about whether they'll be impressed by what you say, or whether they'll use it against you later on. You just ask questions and they answer.

'Is it your birthday too?' I ask.

She shakes her head and points at the teddy.

'I'm sixteen today,' I say, knowing she won't judge me for being a sad sack drinking in the park by myself.

'Oh, you're older than him – he's only two, but that's in bear years. Would you like a piece of cake?'

I nod and she takes a blunt toy knife and hacks away at the sponge until the bit she sliced off for me is just crumbs, which I shovel into my mouth with eager, grubby fingers. She's perfect, this little girl, her golden blonde hair held back by a hairband, and clear intelligent eyes. And the way she moves.

It's so neat and precise, like she knows exactly what she wants, and what she needs to do to get it. She's going on about books and shit as if I know what she's talking about, pausing every now and then, in case either me or the cuddly toy has something to add.

She says something funny – proper funny, not just kiddy funny – and I throw back my head and laugh. That's when I see the woman rushing towards us across the playground, with hair the same shade as my new friend's, and she's got her eyes, too. But that look on her face, rage, bitterness, it hits me full in the face as this savage roar rips out of her.

'GET AWAY FROM MY DAUGHTER!'

My face goes hot, hands clenching into fists as I get on my feet.

'Mum, it's *all right*.'The girl speaks through clenched teeth, sounding as angry as I am, but I don't stick around to listen for long. I'm off down the path, faster, faster until my lungs want to give out.

Troy finds me soon after, out of breath in the alleyway behind Zizzi's. I'm leaning back against a wheelie bin, breathing in big gulps of sour pizza fumes, orange and purple flares flashing across the inside of my eyes, when suddenly he's there. He always knows when I'm weak and low, and it doesn't take him long to get under the skin of it.

'It's simple,'he says, and today his voice is sticky like chewing gum, melted in the sun.'There are two types of people in this world – predators and prey. This girl? Prey. Big fluffy squirrel-like prey. Cute food. But her mum – she's a predator,

51

like a cat. All soft fur and sharp claws, just like Tony was.' He laughs and I can feel my hatred of him boiling up my insides. 'You just got chased off by a fucking *cat*, man. And what does that make you? Squeak, squeak, squeak.'

'I'm not a mouse,' I snarl. A memory flashes into my mind – hiding in my wardrobe from Tony, scuttling off into the shadows whenever he was home. I push the thought away. 'I'm *not*. And one day I'll prove it.'

Chapter 6

Ellie

Keiran was wearing a baggy, grey Superdry top, his skinny shoulders faded to nothing in it, but the way he carried his bag of paints you could tell he was strong. He looked around himself, taking in the full graveyard-of-undead-literature atmosphere of the shop.

'Wow. This place is, like, out of a time warp.'

I felt the heat rising in my face. I hadn't thought of Keiran in the shop. I'd just thought about Keiran in my room, which was a totally different prospect. I had taken hours getting it ready, hiding all the girly teddy bear stuff that guys hate, and making it seem tidy but not so immaculate that it looked like I cared what he thought.

My usual problem with men was that I couldn't play games and pretend. I'd just dump the whole of my personality on them at once, in the hope that my kooky charm would blow them away. This had not gone well in the past.

No, this time I was going to be more cautious, take things slowly. So I had carefully prepped my own space, editing out the things I didn't want to show him yet. But in my effort to make over my bedroom, I'd not really thought about the shop. I had got used to rushing through it to the flat with my head down, not paying attention. I had forgotten what it was like to see it for the first time. 'I know, it's old fashioned,' I explained. 'It's Dave's place, you know.'

'It's kind of cool, actually,' he said. 'I'm not into reading or anything like that, but it's nice to know there's still books around. You know, that it's not just all on computers and stuff.'

I suddenly realised how right he was. I'd never thought of it that way. Keiran was so clever and just so emotionally switched on, I could learn so much from him. He wandered over to the shelves, taking arty pictures of some of the older piles of books with his phone.

'Wow, this stuff is *ancient*. What's up here?' he asked, jumping onto the creaky mezzanine steps.

'More books, I think,' I said, 'but I don't know, maybe a door to Narnia?'

Keiran laughed and I felt a clanging sense of triumph inside. If he got my sense of humour I was halfway there.

I followed him up the steep wooden steps, clinging onto the handrail and, yes, checking out Keiran's butt a little bit while I did so.

'Wow, the Esoterica section – what the hell does that mean?' Keiran asked. 'Seriously, there's all these spell books, and runes, and astral projection guides up here, this is amazing.'

I reached the top of the steps and squeezed onto the landing area, where I found myself standing just a few centimetres away from him. It wasn't a move; there genuinely wasn't enough space for us both to be up there. Suddenly, we were so close I could feel his breath soft on my hair. He smelled of shower gel and spray paint, and I could see every close-up detail of his face – the soft hazel eyes, strands of dark hair, the way his mouth turned up at one corner in a kind of half-smile, and a glimpse of blue tattoo peeking out of his collar. I looked up at him; he gazed down at me.

'Who are you?'

Leah's light and gentle voice made me jump. She was standing right behind me, so close that I couldn't actually turn round to see her without one of us falling down the stairs. I was trapped, wedged between the two of them with no space to move. I tried to look over my shoulder to see her face, but I was stuck, my eyes just inches from the logo on Keiran's shirt. I could feel the heat of his body, and if I took a tiny step forward, we'd be touching.

But I could feel Leah behind me, too. All proud angles and stiffness. They were both taller than me. I imagined their eyes meeting over the top of my head. I felt like sandwich filling.

'Oh, hi. Ellie's my sister's friend,' Keiran said. 'She wants me to paint a mural in her room. I'm . . . OK, it sounds wanky, but I'm a street artist.' He ducked his head down modestly.

'You do graffiti?' Leah's silvery voice had that mocking tone in it, but it was gentler than when she used it on me. Still rude though.

'Not graffiti, no.' Keiran laughed. 'Murals. Some of them are commissioned by people like Ellie here, others I give to the world for free. Like Banksy, only I'm a lot cheaper.'

'What's Banksy?'

'Surely you've heard of Banksy? He's like, the foremost street artist of our time. Although I think his work has got slightly clichéd, personally.'

I fidgeted uncomfortably, and Leah apologised, stepping lightly aside and cramming her slim body into a narrow gap between the bookcases, hung with a tatty yellow curtain. 'You'd better climb down, there's not really room for three people up here.'

I went down first. Behind me, Leah was going on to Keiran about Picasso, and how he became really good at painting realistic pictures before he started doing all those crazy abstract ones. 'I think you need to know all those rules of art before you can break them, don't you agree?' she said.

'Um, I suppose so.' Keiran sounded overwhelmed. 'Anyway, better go check out Ellie's space.'

'It's a straightforward medium,' Leah said. 'Paint on wood-chip wallpaper.'

A Leah joke – she wasn't destined for a career in comedy. Keiran and I both laughed in a polite way.

As soon as my bedroom door was closed, I apologised, rattling on about how she could be prickly sometimes.

'You know, she's the girl who . . .'

'Yeah. I know,' Keiran said. 'Actually, she seemed nice. She had some good points and obviously knows something about art. Funny she hadn't heard of Banksy, though. Anyway, let's see the space. So, this blank wall over your bed – is this it?' He glanced at my window, looking worried. 'That window doesn't look like it even opens.'

I'd never tried – it was draughty enough with it closed.

'I won't be able to use spray paints in here, not without gassing everyone. It'll have to be paint and brushes. And I see what she meant about the woodchip. Hmm ...'

He sat next to me on the bed, the mattress creaking and pushing us closer together, so that his hip was touching mine. I told him about the vlog and he sketched a few ideas out on an artist's pad. A simple, subtle design that could also be adapted into a logo for the site, a whole world conjured up in just a few lines. Keiran talked about colour and light, and the way they worked together in the way that my muso ex-boyfriend used to talk about Nirvana. I wished I could feel that way about something.

'I don't want to go all dorky fan-girl on you, but you are super-talented,' I said. And I meant it; I wasn't just flattering him.

Keiran flushed in an *aw-shucks* kind of way and then for a moment our eyes actually locked.

My body reacted instantly, prickles of excitement on the back of my neck, insides like jelly. If ever there was the time to be the Glitter Queen, going out and grabbing what I wanted, this was it. But to my utter shame I'd never made the first move in my life before.

What if it went wrong? I'd have to face him at Gloria's every other weekend. *Oh God, he might even tell her that I'd thrown myself at him ...*

But what if I didn't, and it never happened?

There was a light tap at the door, and Leah's muffled voice saying hello.

Keiran sprang to his feet a little too quickly, calling for her to come in.

The door opened a crack. Her slim shadow cut a silhouette in the hallway light. She was wearing a baggy loose-knit black jumper – which came down off one shoulder, showing a thin black bra strap – with a pair of leggings and slouchy brown socks. She didn't seem like a normal person; she looked like a character out of a romantic comedy who was having a night in with a tub of ice cream and an old movie.

'Sorry to disturb,' she said. 'I just wanted to tell Keiran sorry for being a bit of an arse earlier. I found this downstairs and thought I'd give it to you, to apologise.'

She held out her peace offering shyly, hesitantly. It was a book, of course. Stokes only ever give books as presents. This one was an old glossy number from the 1980s on Picasso. The cover was slightly sun damaged and it was heavy enough to break a toe if dropped to the floor.

'Thanks,' Keiran said, smiling. He seemed genuinely chuffed.

After a few moments of awkward chat, Leah faded back out through the door, but after that Keiran was full of questions. What school did she go to? Did she ever hang out with Gloria and me? He thought she must be really intelligent, being able to talk about art at the drop of a hat like that.

All the excitement seeped out of my body as I answered his questions and Keiran struggled to keep the fascination out of his voice. A kind of tide of dullness swept over me. Why would he be even vaguely interested in me? I was a boring, immature idiot who didn't know anything about Picasso and faffed about with glitter in my spare time. I was nothing. And Leah had shown him that, in less than five minutes of conversation. I couldn't get over the feeling that I had lost something, without ever getting a chance to find out if it was a thing worth having.

'What an absolute bitch.'

After Keiran left (with a peck on the cheek, and a promise to return soon with a plan but no suggestion of meeting for coffee in the meantime), I'd lost no time calling Billie to moan. I perched on the bedroom windowsill with my back pressed against the chilly window. I had discovered this was the only place I could get a signal.

'Well, it doesn't sound like she spoiled things deliberately,' Billie started to say. But how could she not know? You never disturb a friend when there's a male guest in her room, surely we're all taught that at school or something. It's a basic rule of the Sisterhood.

'You said yourself she doesn't get out much, Ellie.'

'It's the sort of thing everyone knows.'

'I don't think she meant it.'

I nearly fell off my perch – I couldn't believe what I was hearing. I'd supported Billie through the most hysterical rows with her ex, stood up for her when she completely lost it over Luke Besling. And now she was playing the mature, sensible one? This was not why I'd called her. I let my voice go all cold and lofty like Leah does. 'I think you need to reconsider your opinion, as a friend.'

'I think you need to get over yourself!'

So that was Billie. I wasn't going to call Gloria, it was slightly too close to home for that. I heaved myself off the windowsill, stuck my feet into my fluffy slippers and stomped into the kitchen.

'Mum, can I talk to you?'

She was holding up a ladle of pasta sauce to David's lips so he could taste it. Ugh.

'Not right now, Ellie, I don't want to burn the tea.'

'It's urgent. This place is ruining my life.'

David looked at me, shocked, and Mum's facial expression turned to Fake Outrage as she told me not to be so rude. A tiny part of my brain was screaming at me to stop, but I had a choice – tears or yelling – and no way on earth was I going to cry in front of David.

'Why doesn't anybody listen to me? I hate it here!'

Back in my room, I found some angry music and put it on loud so I could have a good scream into my pillow without anyone knowing. Mum was loved-up with David, and Dylan was in a world of his own now his online gaming was up and running again. My friends couldn't even begin to understand what it was like to live here. I felt so lonely, and so pathetic for being lonely.

Without giving it much thought, I dabbed my eyes dry, mounted the video camera on the tripod and arranged it with a tight focus on my face, so you couldn't see the bland, boring room behind me. Once the red blinking light was on, I started to speak.

Hi there, DBLG fans. It's me – and this time I'm here to talk to you about something serious. Like, do you ever feel like a stranger in your own home? . . .

I wasn't stupid. I didn't break any of the Rules – no real names. No discussion of Leah and David's special circumstances. I just talked about how strange it was that when two people fall in love, the people around them have to become a family. How bizarre it is to be sharing a toothbrush mug with someone you'd barely known until a few months ago, to be averting your eyes from your new dad's too-short sleep shorts at the breakfast table. And that funny off-kilter feeling you get when your mum reaches over and affectionately strokes the back of this man's neck, smiling at him with a look so full of love – while you feel nothing for him at all.

Home should be a place where you can be yourself, where people understand you and back your corner, even when you're being crazy and stupid, and throwing glitter over everything in sight. And right now, I feel a long way from home.

I didn't edit it, just uploaded like a strip-down challenge – fidgeting in my chair as David's Wi-Fi was strained to the limit. My eyes and throat were still sore, but I felt calmer, the way I always do when I've talked something through with a friend.

I slithered off the bed and set about putting my room back to the way it was, before I'd made it Keiran-ready. Opening the stiff, creaky drawer under my ancient wardrobe, I started pulling out all the teddy bears, decorative cushions and *Friends 4 Life* picture frames I'd hidden, scattering them across the floor in a huge pile.

What was the point, though, I wondered, looking at the sorry little collection. It wasn't like I'd ever make this place home. It would always be Leah's old room, not mine. I'd always be the pain-in-the-arse girl who loved attention and didn't like books, and she'd always be the spotless, gentle saint who everyone worried about.

I shoved the drawer back into place. The wardrobe creaked and teetered dangerously, but it wouldn't shut.

'Nothing in this place works,' I grunted, slamming it harder, but it wouldn't budge. Peering into the empty space where the drawer was supposed to go, I could see that I'd somehow dislodged a plank of wood at the back and it was now sticking up, stopping the drawer from sliding back in. I reached inside and tried to push it back into place but as I did my fingers brushed something fuzzy. I flinched back in horror, thinking it could be a dead mouse, but after a couple of panicky breaths I realised it was too nylon-textured for that – it must have been a stray plushy. I glanced over at my pile – all furry friends were present and correct.

As I peered closer, I realised that someone had deliberately removed one of the planks and shoved something underneath, then tried to nail it back into place. *Ohmigod, an actual secret panel.*

I pushed my fingers under the loose plank, grabbed a hank of fur and pulled.

There was a sickening rip, but whatever it was came free. I drew my arm out and looked at my prize.

It was greyish-brown, under a thick fuzz of dust, and its limbs flopped loosely forward. I turned it round and saw brown beady eyes, a sad little teddy bear face, torn slightly on its ear where it had got caught in the wardrobe. The same generic sort of bear all of us has had at one time or another and quickly grown out of. But this one had had a lot of love, I could tell by the bare patches and saggy stuffing.

There was a gap in his belly where the stitches had come apart completely, and whoever the owner was – I realised it was probably Leah – had fastened it together again with a rusty old heart-shaped brooch. It was weird to think of her with this thing; it gave me the creeps for some reason. I knew my own collection of soft toys was larger than it should be for a person my age, but that was because people had given them to me. Each one was a memory: a fairground trip with Dad, a jokey sixteenth-birthday gift from Gloria. They meant a lot, but I didn't actually hug them or tuck them up in bed with me. I squeezed the toy's stomach, wondering if it would squeak, but instead, it rustled.

Yes, I did feel guilty as I undid the catch on the brooch, but it didn't stop me. I opened up the gap in the bear's belly and pulled out a tight wad of lined paper. Cool, I thought. A secret diary.

There was a moment's hesitation before I unfolded the pages. I knew that I should have rolled it all up and put it back, then found some way to give it back to Leah, or even destroyed it. But I was never really going to do any of those things. This was my room now, and David had said I could read anything in this house that I liked.

I unfurled the papers, flattened them out in front of me as best I could, and started to read.

After a few pages I reeled back. Then I stared at them, checking I hadn't been mistaken.

By page five, I had to run to the bathroom and be sick.

Chapter 7

Leah

It takes half an hour of searching in the art section but eventually I find a book called *Wall And Piece*, and I have a flick through and get up to date on Banksy. Spray paint. Stencils. Politics. Anonymity. Got it. I hate not knowing about something.

Still, there's an unsettled feeling inside. I distract myself by propping the Banksy book in the window, but it's there, crawling under my skin – the sensation that I've put a foot wrong. I don't have a problem with Ellie's anger, but what bothers me is that I know she has a point. I saw the nervy way they jumped up off the bed when I walked in. I saw that boy's eyes slide away from her and onto me and the look of loss on her face, but I didn't pick up on the signals, I just smiled at him and gave him a present. If I was the apologising type, I'd say sorry, but maybe it would help to keep her angry with me. It might break her annoying habit of talking to me and trying to make me laugh.

I wonder what Ellie would do if she knew the truth about what I did. Would she try to understand?

No, that girl would go straight to the Nosy Parkers. The thought makes me feel sick. I haven't been afraid of the Nosy

Parkers for a long time, but if they found out what really happened it would change everything.

Every kid goes through a stage of believing in monsters, the shadows cast by your bedside lamp which twist and deform into a dark claw reaching for you. The wind blowing in the trees outside becomes the hiss of a demon. Monsters were real to me even *before*.

And soon *after*, I learned to believe in the Nosy Parkers.

They were attracted by trouble, Dad said. 'Any whiff of it and they're all over you.'

The first few times we drove to the police station, Dad asked me to duck down on the car seat under his coat so that the Nosy Parkers wouldn't see me. I hid under the tartan lining, burrowing into the soft fabric, and imagined them running behind the car on springy legs, their hands grasping and clutching at the air we left behind us, grotesque pink noses instead of heads, spiny with hairs. And sniffing – always sniffing out danger, desperation and despair. That's what we smelled like now.

'They'll try to talk to you and ask you things,' Dad warned me. 'Just ignore them. Don't even look at them. I know it feels rude not to answer but it's not; they're the ones being rude.' They sounded horrifying, and when he didn't think I was listening, when he was talking to our new policeman friends, even more terrifying details came out. They worked for news-papers, websites and television and would worm their way into your life, pop up where you least expected them, and trick you into trusting them. They waved big checked books at you and promised you presents, then stole things that were yours. They loved nothing more than digging in dirt and raking muck.

At the beginning, I didn't make the connection between the Nosys and the whole world knowing about me. I was closed in on myself, boiling with rage and grief. My memories of that time are tightly focused on the things physically close to me – the pressure of Dad's arms around me; being under his coat in the car; the gingham plastic chair cushion; the patterned carpet on the living-room floor as I sat there surrounded by toys. In the background, the chatter of Carey's *Disney Princess Enchanted Tales* DVD on a loop. Dad despised all things princessy but now, looking back, I realise he was afraid to let normal TV play in case I caught a glimpse of the news.

One night I woke up suddenly, sweating from another nightmare. Gathering my dressing gown around me, I wandered downstairs to find Dad slumped at his end of the sofa staring at the TV, the remote held limply in his hands. And on the television screen – my face.

It was a photo of me, Mum and Carey, the one Dad had taken on a trip to the New Forest that summer. Mum's cheek was snuggled against my hair, I could still remember exactly how that felt. Kentucky is tucked under my arm and Carey is wriggling in Mum's grasp; she'd been craning her head to see a pony which was just out of shot.

As the newsreader talked, the picture on the screen changed to a pale, badly lit room, and grey-faced Dad with police on either side of him making an appeal for witnesses to come forward.

'I want to show you this photo, to show you the family we were, and what my daughter and I have lost . . .'

I must have made a sound then because Dad leaped out of his chair like he was on springs and the screen went blank.

He told me that the police were still looking for the bad man, that other naughty people were protecting him.

'I thought that if they could just see us all, what a nice family we are. If they could just see your face . . .' Here, his voice cracked, and he gripped my hand so hard it began to hurt. 'I thought they might change their minds and tell us where he is. Then, the police will lock him in prison where he belongs.'

Years later, Dad would explain that that was the day he signed away our privacy for the sake of catching Crow. The picture did the trick – within hours the whole country was talking about us, and within weeks Crow was in custody. But something else happened in the process: I became public property – a national treasure, or a sweetheart, or something. The Face of Courage. People wrote letters and, encouraged by Kentucky's face in the picture, sent teddy bears by the truckload.

'We can't fight this,' he told me finally. 'We have to make it mean something.' That's where CAREY eventually came from – we sold our stories to the newspapers and TV shows that wanted them, moved into the shop and then started the charity.

And so we began to work with the Nosys. It was easier for me than it was for Dad, I had grown used to telling people what they wanted to hear. To smiling when I sensed someone needed a smile, politely accepting a teddy bear, pretending to be a nice, normal little girl. They weren't so scary or so bad. I even got to know some of them a little better: the woman with the sincere voice who said 'Oh, I know. Oh, abso*lutely*' after each of Dad's answers; the funny one with the khaki trousers and bitten fingernails and the short, loud-mouthed photographer with the spiky gelled hair and the big smile. He was a favourite; somehow, he always knew what to say to help me relax.

Recording for TV was strange. I'd sit on a brightly coloured sofa under hot studio lights, so that presenters with great hair and bright shift dresses could tell me how brave I was.

I remember one visit to a TV studio in particular. The interview was pretty standard: same sort of great-hair woman as always, sincere and polite. Afterwards she beamed her thanks at us, handing me a beautifully wrapped package as a thank-you gift. My expert hands squeezed it in a few places and established that, yes, it was another teddy bear.

Then, as we left the set, I noticed an image flickering on a computer screen nearby. I froze, and let my hand slip out of Dad's.

It was the police mugshot of Him. He was gaunt, shaven-headed, his eyes two desperate hollows ringed in red, and mouth tiny and pinched together – every inch the killer. That wasn't how he'd looked the first time I saw him. What he'd done to Mum and Carey had stripped away the shy smile; his furry-caterpillar eyebrows didn't look so funny now. Or maybe he'd just been hiding his true self from me all along.

Dad's hand squeezed mine, giving it a gentle tug. 'I'm sorry you had to see that. Are you OK?'

On the train home we had a carriage to ourselves and Dad explained to me in a quiet voice that the bad man was in prison now. A judge and jury had found him guilty and locked him away for a very long time.

'How long?' A hundred years sounded about right.

'Long enough,' Dad said. 'He's not fully grown up, so he'll go to a special place for boys who've gone wrong in life. They'll straighten him out.'

I stared out of the window, watching the scenery flash past – grey industrial estates and heaps of rubbish, brick archways and grimy buses.

'Do you think he saw us this morning?' I asked. 'Or maybe he read about us in that magazine from last week?'

Dad shook his head and explained that the bad man didn't know how to read. It was part of why his life had gone so wrong. Besides, Dad added, the prison officers probably wouldn't let him watch us on TV or show him pictures of us in magazines.

I imagine he told me those things to reassure me, but as he spoke I realised that all along I'd been hoping he *would* see me. I wanted to know I could speak to him, to pass on a message somehow in a secret language only we understood.

But perhaps I didn't need the magazine to do that. Maybe all I needed to do was to write him a letter or draw a picture, then concentrate on it really, really hard and he would see the message through my eyes.

Back home I took a notebook and pens to my secret hiding place, chose the brightest bloodiest red I could find and started to draw. Chaos flooded out of that pen, terrible thoughts and acts and feelings. I hoped that I could reach him somehow, that he could see them too, and that he would be afraid.

Chapter 8

Boyd, before

Brushing back my hair I feel it, a dry crusted patch of something stuck to my face just next to my hairline. I rub it away. It's his blood, not mine.

I still see flashes of what happened on the estate this morning. The kid's face when he turned the corner into the stairwell and clocked me looking up at him, the way he turned and scrambled away. I grabbed his ankle, wrenched it up, landed two punches in his gut before he even had a chance to fight back.

'Keep hitting,' Bart snarled. I tightened my fist and landed a punch to his jaw. The kid's head recoiled back onto the step with a thud, and for a second I drew back, remembering my instructions: *beat him, don't kill him.*

'KEEP HITTING!' Bart's voice had become a shriek. He'd seen what I hadn't – the kid's fist forming, then shooting up, slamming me in the neck, crushing my windpipe. I choked but managed to hit him again, before jumping to my feet and using my boots. Harder. Harder. Until instinct told me he wasn't going to move any more.

He was shuddering, struggling to breathe as I leaned down and delivered the message: 'This is our fucking postcode.'

I realised my mouth was full of spit and blood where I'd bitten my cheek. I didn't want to swallow, make myself look nervous, so I spat on him. As I did it, the boy's face changed from fear and exhaustion to rage and disgust. I could see his strength surging back up as I landed another kick and ran.

I was the winner – this time.

Now, in the quiet of the library, I look down at my hand, stretching and flexing the fingers, feeling the stiffness and tenderness around the knuckles. Did I go too far? Or maybe I didn't go far enough. I wonder when I'll figure it out, when I'll be a proper enforcer, not just an odd-job bloke.

'You should have kept hitting,' Bart says.

I wave him away with my hand as I see her now, the golden girl I followed in here.

She's wandered off into a quiet corner of the library. Not the kids' section I notice, where her cross-faced mum is trying to keep her squirming sister under control. There's a whole group of screaming toddlers gathered together, as some poor librarian tries to sing nursery rhymes at them. But my girl isn't there, she's wandered into the adult section where they keep all the thick, heavy books and is flicking through one that must be about art, with bright splashy paintings on the cover. Golden Girl is so fucking smart.

Next to her is the rucksack as usual. She reaches inside and pulls the teddy bear out, shushing him elaborately. I walk past, casual like, letting her see me.

'Oh hello,' she says in a quiet library voice. 'Kentucky, look who it is!'

She waves the bear's paw at me, and I wish my others were as friendly and kind as hers. I bet Kentucky never wakes her up in the morning hissing in her ear that she's a stupid waste of space.

'You wouldn't say that if Troy was here,' Bart sneers. I shake my head, as if I could make him tumble out of my ears and slither away, but I know it won't work. I tried it once with a hammer: wound up in hospital with stitches, the worst fucking headache in history, and the others – who now hated me more than ever – plotting to squeeze me out for good.

That's how life works: Golden Girl gets a teddy bear in her head; I get a bunch of psychos.

'Are you OK?' she asks, head to one side. I sit down next to her between the shelves, high-five the bear and tell her I'm fine. It's true, her voice makes them all go quiet.

She shows me the art book she's looking at. The words are just black spiders on the pages as usual, but she knows them all, not even noticing that I'm not reading along. Some of the pictures kind of glow though, and I let it all wash over me, until the group over by the kids' area starts on a loud version of 'The Wheels On The Bus'. Golden Girl groans.

'I hate rhyme time, it's so *babyish*,' she says. 'But stupid Mum and Carey make me come here every week in the holidays.' She goes on, talking about all the annoying things they do.

'Carey breaks everything I care about. The other day I painted this picture of Kentucky. It took me *literally hours*. I didn't just use brown paint, I used three different shades of brown and grey, and got his fur looking really furry. It's the best picture I've ever painted, but then Carey found it and ripped it up, laughing. Mum didn't even care, she just put her hands on her ears and shook her head. She told me to stop whining.' Golden Girl looks at me, head cocked to one side, all thoughtful.

'Do you live on your own?'

I nod – although this is a lie. There's a faded ghost on my living-room couch. Goes by the name of Mum.

'I can't wait to be a grown-up and move out. Sometimes I wonder what it would be like to live all by myself.'

'You could come and live with me,' I say, half meaning it. All sorts of thoughts fly into my head, about how I'd decorate Kyle's old room for her, paint his old bed pink, take her to the park, drop her off at school – the kind of school with a nice smart uniform and no puffy jackets.

This is too much for Troy – he laughs out loud and the sound escapes from my lips.

'That wasn't your voice,' she says. Her eyebrows are dark shot through with blonde, and they're scrunched together in the middle with confusion. I'm so stunned by how clever and right she is, my eyes start to fill with tears.

I want to tell her everything then, about Mum and Tony, and especially Kyle.

That kid. He was golden too, he got Mum's attention in a way I never could. Not that I was jealous because we both got the benefit. He made her make pancakes once – actual pancakes! He just went on and on at her until, one afternoon, when Tony was out, she just did it. I looked the recipe up online while Kyle rummaged around in the cupboards until he found a mixing bowl. She got really into it after a while, whisking until her arm ached and flipping bits of batter at Kyle. But the best bit was the tossing – three pancakes went on the floor before she got the hang of it, and all three of us were laughing as we brushed off the grubby bits and layered chocolate spread on them.

So yes, Kyle had a way of making her do things that were good for both of us.

'It's you and me, bro,' he used to say as if he were the older one. He *should* have been the older one. I did a shit job of protecting him.

Over in the kiddy section, the singing has stopped and the mum is getting up off the floor and stretching her legs stiffly. I melt backwards between the bookshelves so she can't see me. A grown man smeared with blood talking to a pretty blonde girl? I'm not a perv – in fact, if someone tried that with her I'd gut them alive – but I know how it looks.

'See you around, kid and bear,' I say.

She nods, glancing over at her mother with complete understanding.

I really do want to take her home, keep her close, get her to tell me where the others end, and I begin. But it isn't a plan, just a stupid wishful thought floating through the air. Something that should never go further than that.

Chapter 9

Ellie

The mural was beautiful, with splashes of colour and dots of light here and there that made the whole thing leap off the wall like it was three dimensional. But I wondered if I'd ever be able to look at it without thinking about this day.

About how Keiran turned up with Billie and Gloria in tow. Watching them troop through the shop made me feel like he'd organised a parade under a big hurtful banner saying, NOT INTERESTED.

About the way I tried to make the best of things, fired up my party playlist and poured out a bag of Doritos in a bowl for everyone to share. I laughed loudly at every joke. I stuck Doritos under my top lip and pretended to be a vampire. I composed a spontaneous, witty song about Gloria's latest crush. I felt hollow.

Nothing I said or did could tame the mess of emotions sloshing around inside me. First, there was the shame, a kind of dull throb in my guts caused by the fact that Keiran was clearly not into me, and that Gloria and Billie knew it. But that part was pretty standard, almost boring, compared to the flood of panic I felt every time I thought about the drawings I'd found.

God, those drawings.

There were pages of them. Simple kids' stuff – 2-D figures with arms and legs sticking out at the sides, wearing lumpen skirts and angular trousers.

But the faces. Instead of the basic smile, they were twisted: dot-like eyes wide open, teeth bared in pain or anger or horror. So much red felt tip.

Blood flowed everywhere. And in every scene: a smiley-faced blonde girl in a pink princessy dress with puffy sleeves – holding a knife.

Each drawing had a title scrawled across the top, in the blue sky next to the clouds, in childish handwriting, with cheery round blobs on the 'i's.

I will find you. I will get you. I will make it hurt.

Since I'd found them, everything I'd ever believed about Leah had shifted. I once thought the way she moved was graceful and natural, but I saw through it now. Every gesture she made in public was tightly controlled, even more fake than me – the person who took an apple to a gig to get attention. Even the way she'd eaten breakfast that morning, nibbling her muesli, elbows tucked into her sides, cleaning the spoon a shiny silver with each mouthful; just like a model in a luxury yoghurt advert. Like she'd seen that this is how people enjoy food, and she was imitating it as best she could. She was always together, always poised and always completely false.

I still felt sorry for her, of course I did. But now I was afraid of her, too.

Keiran was nearly finished when I caught sight of movement at the bedroom door. Leah watching us through the crack, her face ghostly, expressionless.

I jumped. She always made me jump now. She gave me a cold stare.

'Come and join us,' Billie said. 'We've got way more crisps than the four of us should eat. Go on, Ellie, tell her to stay.'

I shrugged. 'She can if she wants.' *Please don't.*

Quietly, gracefully and without saying a word, she gave a little half-smile and drifted away. I felt like a tense fist in the middle of my chest had relaxed, until I turned back to my friends and saw their faces.

'That was harsh,' Billie said.

She seemed so nice, they told me. Why hadn't I introduced them? Why was I being so rude?

'She's fine,' I said, snappish and defensive. 'She's not into crowds. She doesn't really like . . . people.' I wasn't lying. From what I'd seen in that teddy bear, she really didn't like people – especially not policemen, a lady in a brightly coloured waistcoat and a man with big furry eyebrows. No, she didn't like people at all, although she did seem to like knives quite a lot.

After I'd told Keiran how wonderful the mural was about a million times, and we were all standing around chatting, Gloria grabbed my elbow and led me aside into the family room. She told me she understood that it's not easy being in a stepfamily, and to give it time. 'Keiran's all right now but he was a complete fucker for the first year. You need to give Leah a chance. Stop acting so weird around her, don't be so jealous.'

Jealous?

I pulled my arm away and stared. Is that what everyone thought?

'That stepfamily vlog,' she said. 'Well, it was a bit *intense*.'

I was on steadier ground here. It'd had loads of views and positive comments from people in the same boat as me and even a few mentions from bigger YouTubers. I wasn't alone – there were people out there who understood. 'It's one of the most popular things we've done so far. I'm not taking it down.'

'I know, I know, but maybe you ought to let things settle for a while?'

I opened my mouth to reply but I had no idea what to say, and then Gloria was swept away on a tide of goodbyes. As my friends walked away across the sticky pavement, I saw Gloria link arms with Billie and her murmured words drifted back towards me: 'I tried. Give her time.'

I knew what I should do: take the higher path, move on and forget what I'd seen on those screwed-up bits of paper. It was the sensible, wholesome thing to do. Be the bigger person. Instead, I decided to spy on my stepsister.

As I tiptoed down to the bookshop after hours, I was completely aware that I was being stupid. I already regretted looking at those notes and drawings – what good would it do me to find out any more of her secrets? And yet I wasn't going to turn back.

Over the past few weeks, I had looked everywhere in the flat – the box-room, the filthy ladder leading up to a terrifying, decaying attic, and even David and Mum's wardrobe. I'd found no trace of a Leah bed, or a Leah room. *Maybe she sleeps hanging upside down from the rafters,* I thought sarcastically, and for once I didn't find myself funny. No, it had to be somewhere in the shop. So I crept downstairs.

I was prepared for the darkness, but I hadn't been prepared for the alive feeling the shop had at night. The stacks seemed to loom over me and fold me in.

My phone torch was broken, so I had grabbed one of Dylan's bike lights. I flicked it on and the book spines around me lit up in shadowy pools of red. Not the best choice of bike light.

A creaking footstep made my heart slam against my ribcage. But it was overhead, probably from the kitchen. Mum and David were learning to bake bread together, another thing that was apparently more fun than television. Dylan was out at a friend's and Leah was in the lounge doing her homework. There was no point waiting until she was out as she only went out one evening a week. A mysterious Thursday-night errand that brought her back after a couple of hours looking flushed, tired and glittery-eyed. The rest of the time she was at school, or here.

The light glinted on a nail sticking out of the mezzanine staircase. Of course, her hideaway had to be up there on the creaking death trap. For a better grip, I shuffled out of my badly fitting ballet flats and kicked them to one side on the dusty floor before climbing slowly, my socks catching on the splinters, until I reached the top.

The light slid over modern, coloured spines and older battered ones, with glimmering gold lettering and obscure titles. *Paganism. Wicca. Spells for Beginners. The Unexplained.* Oh yes, just as David said, all the best stuff was kept up here.

And there it was. The narrow gap between bookshelves with the dingy, patterned curtain hanging across it. It seemed so obvious now, but I'd only been up here once, and Keiran had distracted me. Now I understood why she'd appeared so quickly and seemingly out of nowhere on that day.

Paranoid, I scratched at the bookcase and whispered, 'Leah, are you in there?'

After three heartbeats, I pushed inside. It was so narrow I could only just squeeze through.

A sad, saggy little mattress, scrunched-up layers of quilt, sheets and blankets, thrown aside where she'd got out of bed. Like a homeless person's camp that you'd find under a bridge, or in a bus shelter. On the wall behind, there were layers of tattered photographs and magazine clippings. I had a pinboard like it upstairs, full of pouting, grinning selfies of friends on girls' nights out, ticket stubs, flyers and festival wristbands. But Leah's was all magazine clippings and post-cards – photos of Brazilian beaches, rainforests and Rio. Like a wall of wishful thinking. Pinned among the photos was a little square of blue-checked plastic fabric, and the slip of cream satin I'd seen her cut away from the wedding dress. I thought about Leah and the knife again and shuddered.

As I turned away, I noticed a battered old suitcase that she seemed to be using as a bedside table. There was a tiny key sticking out of the lock, with a pink ribbon threaded prettily through it.

I shouldn't . . .

I did.

Inside it, my red light fell on more battered notebooks, pages crunchy where she'd pressed the paper so hard with her biro. There was a tattered Bible, full of bookmarks, and as I flicked through I noticed all the violent bits were underlined. A pressed flower marked one particular page, which was about God sending plagues.

I tucked it back into the box gently, trying to keep everything where it was. As I did, my fingers brushed a brown envelope stuffed with newspaper clippings and internet printouts. I sank from a kneeling position down onto the mattress and gently lifted them out. Confetti pieces of decayed newspaper fluttered out onto the bedsheet. *Shit*.

I thought they'd be her own clippings – interviews she'd given over the years, photo shoots, reviews of the *Book of Hope* she'd 'co-authored' with David when she was fifteen. But they were all about Crow. The bloke who did it, the killer.

I'd never really given the guy much thought. But of course Leah thought about him, of *course* she did. I realised now who the 'he' was in her scribblings, who the furry-browed figure in the pictures was, and why he was being sliced and diced. Carefully, I slid the cuttings back into the envelope, then lifted the mattress and brushed the bits of crumpled paper underneath.

Then there were the notebooks. Lifting them gently out, I opened a page at random and read:

> *The trachea. A blow to the windpipe can wind and shock him and slow his reactions. A severe blunt or penetrating trauma can cause death by airway obstruction or exsanguination. (NB: Check how severe!!)*

Leah's handwriting had improved, I noticed, feeling strangely detached. It was much less scribbly than mine – probably, Mum would say, because Leah took the time to think about what she wrote, rather than just scrawling it out like silly old me. I pictured Leah, taking time over this. Carefully choosing her words and noting everything down with precision, description after description of violent and painful deaths. They were more organised than the old scribblings I'd found, as if the thoughts in those early drafts hadn't ever gone away, just grown up. They weren't childhood fantasies any more, they were plans.

At that moment, I heard the sticky-up floorboard in the hallway upstairs creak loudly, which meant someone was heading down towards the shop. My insides lurched in panic. I shoved the diary back into the case. Then I flicked off the light, grabbed my torch. It took seconds to slip back through the curtain, but I was trapped on the mezzanine. All I could do was tread lightly to the next row of bookcases and tuck myself between them. I crouched down as low as I could, pressing myself back into the dark recesses.

A footstep on the mezzanine steps. Light as a feather. I pushed further back, a sharp book spine dug into my back. Dust tickled my nose. My lip hurt. I realised I was biting it hard, trying to stay still so much that I was shaking. I worried I was breathing too loudly, so I stopped breathing.

Leah bounded up the steps, agile as a monkey, without needing to put the shop lights on. She moved like some of the dancers in my class, on the balls of her feet, barely making an impact as I heard her pull the curtain aside.

She was only in there for a few moments before she emerged. I glimpsed her outline, with what looked like a textbook tucked under her arm as she swung back down the stairway. I breathed out slowly but stayed frozen still, unable to tell if she'd gone back upstairs to the living room or was still below me in the shop. I waited for five minutes, but then pins and needles crept into my foot. I told myself I was being silly, stretched my leg out and wiggled my toes.

Over in the corner of the shop I heard a whisper of movement, a release of breath, oh so quiet: 'Hmmm.' There were light footsteps on the stairs, the creak of the hallway floorboard, then nothing.

It wasn't until I got to the bottom of the steps that I remembered my stupid damn ballet flats were waiting there for me in full view.

*   *   *

I scuttled back to my room and waited. Would Leah report me to Mum and David? Their muffled laughs drifted along from the kitchen, wafted on a smell of freshly baked bread. No outrage, anger and parental disappointment was coming my way yet. Would she – and this was worse – *deal with me herself?*

Shaking, I opened my laptop and looked up exsanguination online: death by blood loss. Lovely. It took a few moments to barricade my bedroom door with a chair, then I went back and looked up Crow.

All I knew about him was what the leaflets had told me, which summed him up in three words: troubled gang member. It all sounds so simple in the CAREY literature, like a formula which adds up into one thing: poverty + drugs + mental illness = psycho killer. If we could just minus all those things, we'd have no psycho killers at all. Mum said that the charity deliberately focused on the broken society and poverty that had made Crow into a killer, rather than the kid himself, but that still put him in a neat little box: helpless kids who can only be saved by rich people with time on their hands.

The CAREY office was always full of volunteers helping stuff envelopes or hit people up for money on the phone. I wondered how many of them had bought drugs off people just like Crow at some time in their lives, feeding money into the problem.

At the tender age of sixteen, Crow had already had several brushes with the law, the newspaper website said. He'd been a year younger than I was now when he'd taken that knife and hidden out in that shopping centre car park. Before then it was all broken home, broken family, drugs and debt. A tall skinny loser of a lad called Boyd White who had drifted into the local gang on his estate, the Factory Crew. He'd got himself mixed up in muggings and drug deals, took to dressing all in black and calling himself Crow. I read that it wasn't normal for the papers to name an underage offender like him, but they'd got special permission, saying it was in the public interest. Then they'd just called him Crow all the time anyway, probably because it sounded much scarier than Boyd.

I wondered if the other gang members had sniggered at the nickname behind his back. They'd certainly used him for all their dirtiest jobs, paid him nothing and let the drugs eat his brain. That's what must have happened to Boyd, because there was no sense in what had happened to Jane and Carey. I found lots of panicky articles about the MENACE OF SKUNK, describing how some users went on to develop mental health issues and in the end he'd been sentenced for manslaughter because his life and his brain had been such a mess when it happened.

Everything I read was so full of fear and panic. There were words like *crazy* and *psycho* and, after the manslaughter decision, anger from people who thought he should be jailed for life for cold-blooded murder.

Only one article was different, an anonymous barrister's blog, saying that public hysteria had swayed the judge and jury, that jail was the wrong place for him and he needed hospitalisation. It felt right, reasonable . . .

. . . But then he'd stabbed two people. He'd killed a *child*.

I leaned back from the laptop, dizzy, different thoughts clashing in my head. Why did reality have to be so *complicated*?

Still, I read on, lost in the horror of what had happened to Jane and Carey.

But not to Leah. *Without a scratch*, the reports all said. Others used words like 'lucky' or, more creepily, 'spared'. But none of them explained why. Most of them presumed he'd been disturbed during the attack, but maybe it wasn't that. What if he'd always intended to leave her unharmed? *What if he'd had other plans for her?*

I closed the screen, tried to detach myself from the story of Boyd White, to stop thinking about what was going on in Leah's brain. I should get back to worrying about everyday things – how to improve our YouTube hit rate, what Mum was going to make me wear to the wedding. I needed to stop now, this was none of my business.

But what happened to Leah was real, important and horrifying, and my own petty insecurities and issues were nothing in comparison. Her problems were an aching, whirling black hole in space. But the harder I tried to pull away, the more I could feel myself getting sucked in.

Chapter 10

Leah

As soon as she is back in her room I return, climbing the steps as fast as I can, pulling the curtain aside and cursing myself for being so stupid. There was my suitcase key, left sticking out of the lock like some trusting idiot. *Always* lock it. ALWAYS. I can't lose everything when I'm so close to getting what I want.

She's so clumsy. I see bits of newspaper cutting on the floor and in my bedside case my diaries are piled up in the wrong order. Which ones did she read? How long was she down here before I caught her at it? How *dare* she?

I lift the envelope of cuttings and my folders of old school-work, and feel through the suitcase lining underneath. My fingers touch the soft worn cotton T-shirt, and the hard shape beneath it. Relief floods through me: it's still there, solid and real. The papers above it look undisturbed, I don't think she got that far down. She probably thinks she's found everything I have to hide, but she is wrong.

I groan and lean back against the wall, swallowing the sob that wants to come out and digging my nails into my hands as hard as I can let them. I don't want any marks that Dad will see. My heart is pulsing fast, my eyes full of tears, my jaw tight and clenched. *This won't do, I can't lose control.* I take deep breaths, the way my kiddie-shrink showed me all those years ago – the only useful thing she ever did teach me. *Breathe. Focus on the breath. One, two, three, four, five.*

It takes me a few moments to realise that it's not just the fact of her nosing around in my plans that's making my stomach clench. It's the thought of her in here, in the only place that makes me feel safe.

When we moved into the shop Dad made a huge effort to give me a dream little girl's bedroom. It smelt of fresh paint – bright, garish pink with colourful stencils of flowers on the wall. Dad had given me a frilly lampshade, a fluffy rug and the cabin bed I had always begged for.

Up on the ceiling, he had done his best to paint over a heart-shaped crack in the plaster. Teddy bears – bears that weren't Kentucky – teemed on every shelf. Generous gifts from well-wishers within the family and complete strangers who had read my story and been moved. Apart from the rickety wardrobe in the corner which had come with the flat, everything was new, new, new.

No dirty marks on the bedside where Carey had stuck rows of Barbie stickers and then cried when I peeled them off. No big awkward drawers that only Mum and Dad were strong enough to open; everything glided on smooth little rails with a soft-close setting. My socks and T-shirts used to smell of the little lavender bags Mum slipped into the drawer with them, now they just smelt of new.

It was a little girl's room, for sweet, well-behaved things who liked ponies or ballet. I did not want it, and I did not deserve it.

'What do you think?' Dad asked.

I told him it was beautiful.

'And do you like the new shop? Exciting, isn't it?'

I told him I hated it. Two lies in one short minute.

I thought I was going to hate the shop. I had planned to stay in my room as much as possible and ignore the growing library downstairs. But as the higgledy-piggledy shelves began to fill with books, I wandered around the maze Dad had created.

'It's got to feel like a treasure hunt,' he told me. 'I loved these shops when I was a kid – when you find the book that's right for you, it feels like a prize.'

I loved the smell of the old print and paper, the worn, retro covers. I'd wander through the shelves, running my grubby fingers over the withered spines as I went, sometimes grabbing one that sounded old, obscure or inappropriate. Stuffy Victorian romances, 1970s books about the life of parasites (with grisly but fascinating full-colour pictures) or aged copies of the *Fortean Times* which promised aliens and ghosts living next door. As I wandered, I'd be transformed myself – I was Sleeping Beauty one day, then the Minotaur, then Hansel and Gretel. Victim, monster, victim.

The outside world was faint, indistinct. New school was the same as old school, full of blurs. The blurry teachers set me work, and I did it without complaining – just enough to get by, not enough to win extra praise or attention. There was no outright bullying. They'd had an assembly before I started and the other children were told an edited version of what had happened to me, and how this was a chance for the school to help me rebuild my life. So nobody picked on me, but nobody wanted to be my friend, either.

It's easy to see why. The whole world is in danger all the time – a bus could run you over, a chunk could fall off a broken building and flatten you. Or a bad man could wait for you in a car park with a knife, and slice you open. The only way we can live with this fear is to tell ourselves it won't happen to us. We're safe because we look when we cross the road. We keep clear of building sites. We don't go near the bad people. And then you see someone like me. Not on TV or in a newspaper, but flesh-and-bone, sitting at the desk next to you. I have the same pencil case as you. My school jumper is frayed at the edges just like yours. Living proof that bad things happen to seemingly normal people. Faced with that kind of truth, it's easier to pretend I'm not there.

Oh, there were a ghoulish few, who asked questions about blood and knives and ghosts. I kept my head down and they soon disappeared. I counted the hours on my pink plastic watch until I could get back to the shop.

And there we waited. Dad behind his shop counter and me hidden in the bookshelves. We waited for life to make sense again.

'It's important work we're doing here,' Dad told me. 'It's what your mum and Carey would have wanted.' But the bookshop was always doomed to be a failed experiment, the charity's predecessor which never quite worked out, and became our home instead. The hordes of troubled young gang members never showed up.

Dad talked about Mum and Carey all the time: how beautiful and funny Mum was, Carey's cute little dimples. It was all true, but he never talked about the real stuff, like the time he gave Carey so many Laughing Cow triangles it made her sick, and Mum yelled and threw the empty box at him. Or Carey's purple-faced, scrunch-eyed tantrums, and the time she screamed the whole way to playgroup because Mum wouldn't let her wear her pink sandals in November. The Mum and Carey he talked about didn't sound like people to me, they were saints. But I said nothing as it hurt me to talk about them, and I couldn't tell him why. I missed them, I missed them so much, the solid reality of them. Two people I could cuddle and poke and tickle and just reach out and grab if I wanted to, because they were mine. I would never have that again.

Because we'd killed them, that strange man and me.

I built a lot of dens during that time. I'd always loved caves, homemade tents in the garden, blanket dens in the living room. But before they'd always been little homes – a picnic area for family meals, a shoebox bed in the back for Kentucky.

Now there was no Carey and Kentucky was just a stuffed toy that I couldn't stand to look at. Now the things I built were definitely closer to forts. They were for hiding in, keeping people out. The shelves of the shop were great for propping blankets up and if I chose a dark enough corner it would be undisturbed by customers for days.

Then one day, as I was carefully constructing a fort on the mezzanine balcony, I pushed aside an ancient pile of *National Geographics* and found a gap behind where the rear panel of the bookcase had come away. Pulling the magazines out, I pushed my head and arms through.

Wow. Behind the shelves was a deep alcove about a metre across. Dad clearly hadn't found a shelf to fit, so he'd arranged the bookcases to form a square around it, leaving a space perfect for me to curl up in.

A thin thread of light filtered in from outside and through the cracks in the mezzanine floor, enough to read by if I strained my eyes. Otherwise it was dark, dusty and gloomy. I loved it.

I squeezed the rest of my body through, reached out and pulled the magazines back into place. I sat there in the darkness for some time, my knees drawn up to my chin on the dusty floor, and I smiled, my facial muscles stiff and creaking with the novelty of it. *Nobody knows I'm here.*

After that, I became an expert in disappearing, melting away between the bookshelves. At first, I was just hiding from Dad and his raw, aching gaze of concern, but as the months passed the reasons to hide just grew and grew. There was the shrink lady with her bright array of crocheted waistcoats, her toy-box full of symbolism and pencil case full of double-edged swords. *Draw me a picture*, she'd say, and our session would stretch out in endless silence, my felt tip pens scratching on the paper and her measured intakes of breath as she saw what I drew.

At the beginning, I drew honestly. I really can't remember what it was that I drew, but there was no violence in the pictures, no gushes of red across the page. I wasn't stupid. But there was still something about the drawings that seemed to disturb her.

Overnight, I switched to aggressively nice. I'd sketch daisies in a row, hand-in-hand chains of smiling stick children running over a grassy field. At the time I thought I was being clever, but the tension still came off her in waves. So I started refusing to go, resulting in endless standoffs that brought Dad to the verge of tears.

Just try dragging a traumatised eight-year-old kicking and screaming into a psychologist's office and you'll understand why he eventually gave up.

I also hid away from the steady trickle of do-gooders who had started to appear at our door. Bored women fending off the pointlessness of their lives by helping Dad stack books in the dodgy part of town. Lonely women looking for other women to chat to. Earnest women who worried about our neglected youth but who didn't actually want to meet any of them. Always women, though. They wanted something from me, my smiles, my gratitude – some cuteness, at least. I tried my best, but sometimes I hid.

I found that the more people there were the easier it was to vanish, while each adult assumed that a different adult was looking after me. If I reappeared when somebody called my name, then nobody really worried about where I had been. And if I told Dad I'd been reading, he'd just smile in that proud chip-off-the-old-block way and ruffle my hair. I learned how easy it was to keep secrets if you just told people what they wanted to hear, how to reply to a question without really giving an answer, and how to do what I wanted, while seeming to do as I was told.

I collected scraps of paper and pictures to decorate the backs of the bookshelves, stacked my most precious books around me, coloured in murals on the walls and stole cushions from the ottoman chest in Dad's room. This was my place – nobody could take it from me.

'Another adjournment?' Dad said into his phone, as I crouched upstairs in my hidey-hole. 'Why? I don't understand.'

I leaned close to the dusty floorboards, pushing my face down so I could see through a convenient crack into the shop below. Dad was pacing and looking over his shoulder to check that I wasn't around. The scrape-scrape of the other voice on the phone was too faint for me to hear. Dad stopped to listen, his whole body clenched up tight. He spoke slowly, in a tone of voice I hadn't heard before. 'I don't care about psychiatric problems, or whatever bullshit story he's come up with. I tried . . . I'm trying to understand, but I want justice, I want this to be over.' Dad's voice cracked. He slammed the phone down onto the counter – it bounced and spun and clattered onto the floor.

And then he sank down onto the chair and collapsed forward, clutching both sides of his head. His neck was bent down, and I could see each white knobble of his spine as his shoulders shook with a few silent sobs. A swallowing, gasping sound came from his throat and he pushed the balls of his hands into his eye sockets, as if trying to shove the tears back in.

I was frozen, helpless. Uncle Jeff, who had been stacking a bookshelf nearby, came and stood next to him, a hand laid on one shoulder.

'I can't even imagine . . .' he began pointlessly.

'I hate him,' Dad said at last. 'I've been having these thoughts, this anger . . . Jeff, I want to kill him. Take his knife, slice him to ribbons, see the fear in his face as I take each cut. It's wrong and it's savage but . . .'

'You can't think like this.' Jeff's soft Mancunian tone was uneasy, reaching for the right thing to say – like Dad had spilled something and he had to persuade him to tidy it up. 'You've got your daughter to think about, and you're really building something here.'

Dad straightened up, he took a deep ragged breath and started pulling books out of a box in front of him.

'You don't know what it's like, Jeff,' he said. 'Pretending not to feel this, being strong. Getting out of bed and making breakfast every. Single. Day. Cleaning the bathroom, paying bills, learning how to braid hair. Without her.' His voice cracked and I felt the pain of loss twisting in my chest too.

There was silence, but for the sound of sorting books and Jeff shifting around uncomfortably. But when Dad spoke again his voice was hard.

'This goes against everything I've ever stood for and I'd never say it out loud to anyone else but . . . he doesn't deserve to live in this world any more. Not after what he did.'

At that moment, Dad took a book from the box and looked at the title, before throwing it lazily across the room with a dry and broken 'hah'.

It skittered under an old library bookcase and stayed there until I pulled it out later that night, when Jeff had gone home and the shop was closed.

It looked like the kind of book I loved, made in the days before we had to have big glossy pictures on the cover to sell a story. It looked like it could have been in Charles Dickens's library, with its red fabric cover and faded gold lettering embossed on the cracked spine: *The Count of Monte Cristo*. It was by the Three Musketeers man so even though it was thick, I knew it would be good. It turned out to be the best book ever.

The next few hours were swallowed up by it, the story of the man thrown into prison for a crime he didn't commit by three evil men, and how he swore to get his revenge. When Dad called me for bedtime, I could hardly tear myself away. I kept it hidden, returning to my hidey-hole to read it whenever I could.

I couldn't stop thinking about it, not even when I was tucked up in bed, staring up at the crack in my bedroom ceiling and feeling afraid to sleep in case I dreamed. When the hands of my Hello Kitty clock slid past 4 a.m., I wriggled out of the sheets, grabbing my pillow and duvet. Stepping carefully over the creaky floorboards and around the piles of books, I crept down to the shop and clambered into the Hole. Swaddled caterpillar-like in my quilt, I read and read until I fell asleep, and for the first time since that day, I didn't dream about Mum and Carey.

Next morning, Dad's crashing feet woke me before his cries did, thudding on the stairs, toppling books and papers as he ran. 'Leah ... Leah ... Oh Christ, LEAH!'

There wasn't time to sneak out; I had to get to him. Snaking the top of my body through the tiny gap, I shouted back, 'Dad I'm all right, I'm here.'

He tore up the wooden steps, saw me coming out of the bookshelf and pulled me through – into that tight hug, that crushing please-be-alive hold. I forced my body to relax until his grip eased. Then the angry phase kicked in and he told me my pyjamas were filthy, and he'd been worried sick, and where had I been?

I pointed at the gap in the shelves, the scattered books and bedding. He could just about fit his head and shoulders in.

'You've been sleeping in here?' Dad was horrified. The place was dirty, cold and draughty. Hadn't I always been afraid of spiders? 'I don't understand, Leah,' he said, shaking his head. 'What's wrong with the bedroom I made for you?'

'I have nicer dreams here.'

There was no further debate, just a few changes. Dad cleaned the place out and moved one of the bookshelves a fraction so that he could squeeze inside – he insisted on that, in case I was ill someday. We hung an old curtain up over the gap so shop customers couldn't see in and found that there was room for a small foam mattress, a warm duvet and plenty of pillows. He even ran an extension cable up through the floor to give me a bedside light.

'If you're cold, you come upstairs. If you get scared, or you just want to sleep in your proper bed,' he told me, 'it's still there waiting for you.'

I never did. Years later, when Dad gave my old room to Ellie, I just moved my clothes into the tiny room at the end of the hall and didn't give it a second thought.

And now she's invaded my refuge. The thought of her greedy, glittery fingers rifling through my things makes me feel sick all over again. Up until now she's been an occasionally amusing minor irritation. But after tonight that has changed.

She is my enemy now.

Chapter 11

Ellie

It was the eyebrow gel that gave it away, that gave me that first uneasy sense of wrongness when I went into my room that afternoon. At first it was just a vague feeling that something was out of place on my dressing table. I dropped my school bag to the floor and took a step closer. Something was definitely off.

I didn't like to admit it – it went against my freewheeling, spontaneous image – but I was really fussy about where I kept my make-up. I'd spent a fortune on a Perspex caddy thing in TK Maxx and everything had its slot – blushers on the left, foundations at the back, brushes in a special pot, lippy and eye make-up all kept in very precise order: left to right, cheapest to most expensive. I knew exactly where everything was. I could stumble out of bed, half-blinded by lack of sleep and a colossal hangover, and still be able to put my hands on the make-up I needed to fix my face.

That's how I knew. No way would I put the Benefit volumiser next to the No7 brow-sculpting pencil.

I sat down at the dressing table to see if anything else had changed, and nearly fell over in the process. My swivel chair was about 10 cm lower than it usually was. Then I reached forward to switch on my fairy lights and nothing happened. They'd been unplugged.

Someone had been in my room.

Normally the first suspect would be Dylan, but this wasn't his style. When Dylan trespassed he wandered in, grabbed a fiver out of my money jar, leaving the loose change trailing all over my quilt and a half-drunk bottle of Coke Zero on the bedside. No touching of make-up or other things that didn't interest him. This was different, deliberate, designed to make me feel uneasy. I'd invaded her space, now she'd invaded mine.

This was Leah.

Glancing up at my noticeboard I saw that one picture – my favourite one of me, Billie and Gloria all looking hot at the No Info gig – was slightly askew, and there was a series of black circles drawn around my face in marker pen, looking almost like a target.

And then I had a horrible thought. With a surge of panic, I leapt up and flung myself onto the floor, reaching under the bed for EXTRA TAMPONS, pulling open the top of the box.

Shit shit shit.

The GoPro was gone.

My fear turned to fury, my heart hammering as heat rose through my body. How dare she?

I stormed out of my room. Friendly, chatty sounds were coming from the kitchen so that's where I went. Mum and David were poring over something CAREY-related on David's laptop, Dylan and Leah were sitting at the table doing their homework, side by side. I felt revolted.

'Give it back,' I said.

Four faces stared up at me, all of them looking shocked and bemused.

'That camera's not just mine,' I blurted, stumbling over my words. 'It belongs to my friends too, so give it back, Leah.'

I know how to fake innocence, I've done it enough times, and Leah's face was textbook – that perfect blend of hurt, outrage, confusion. Not too dramatic either, just understated enough to be believable. Nice.

David's lips were pressed together, twitching, like he was desperate to say something but holding himself back. On the keyboard, his fingers had curled under, bunching up into fists.

'Ellie!' Mum said, shock and shame in her voice.

Leah looked at me, her angelic look still in place, but beneath it I could see she was watching me, waiting. My brain ran ahead down blind alleys of things I wanted to say:

She drew on one of my photos.

She unplugged my fairy lights.

She moved my eyebrow gel.

I could hear how unlikely, how ridiculous and dramatic and, well, *Ellie-ish* it would sound. *It must be your imagination. Why would lovely Leah do anything like that? One of your friends must have done it ...* I hadn't spoken the words but I could already feel the hot humiliation that would come after them.

David's nose wrinkled with disapproval and distaste, Mum's disappointment as she apologised to him on my behalf.

My eyes met Leah's. She raised one eyebrow ever so slightly, a look of such perfect poise and malice that once again my anger turned to fear. She was in control. I'd done exactly what she expected me to do.

I had lost. There was nothing I could say to get Mum on my side, or to protect myself from Leah.

'Sorry, Mum,' I said, 'it's nothing . . . just a mistake . . .'

Hot-faced I ran back to my bedroom, slamming the door behind me just in time for the tears to come. I threw myself on the bed, burying my face in the pillow.

At least now Billie and Gloria might believe me about Leah's weirdness – at least I hoped they would, because it would take ages to save up for another camera. Did Leah even understand the meaning of what she'd taken? I didn't think so – she didn't seem to have a clue about YouTube. But somehow, instinctively, she always seemed to know how to hurt me.

And I had to live with her, 24/7.

A new wave of misery. My body was racked with sobs again. I curled up into a ball, and as I did my knee knocked against a hard lump under my duvet.

Jumping up, I pulled back the covers and there it was. Of course. She would never be so clumsy as to actually steal something. She just wanted me to think it was stolen, to create a fuss, to embarrass myself.

Beneath the GoPro was a folded piece of A4. I unfolded it to find a computer printout, a colour picture of a sign, the kind you see near power stations or deep water – a yellow triangle with black stripes around the outside and in the centre of it, just one word. Her unmistakable but untraceable message to me.

WARNING.

Chapter 12

Leah, thirteen

The sparring gloves felt strange and heavy, rank with other people's sweat and I felt absurd in them. My hands curled up inside, hot and weak, as my instructor, Marc, corrected my stance.

Mixed martial arts: Dad had been horrified when I'd first brought the subject up. It didn't fit with what he thought of me – shy, bookish, cerebral me. Why would I want to spend my spare time hitting things? But I'd talked him round, emphasised the 'arts' aspect of MMA, called it 'updated judo'. I knew he'd had judo lessons as a kid and that they'd given him confidence.

'I just want to feel braver when I'm out and about,' I'd told him, pausing for a moment, letting him imagine me walking the streets in fear, and then I added the clincher: the week before, he'd appeared on a panel with an academic who argued that regular sporting activity would cut juvenile mental health problems in half.

'I think doing a sport would really help me . . . *cope*,' I said, then I handed Dad the number and watched as he made the call.

'What do you want to get out of these lessons?' Marc asked me at our first session. He was a towering hulk of a man with a tight, disciplined way of moving which wasted no unnecessary energy. He had a way of looking at your body and knowing exactly what each and every muscle was doing – *think about those glutes . . . keep your balance . . . what the hell are you doing with your core?* I wanted to impress him, and I knew that telling him I was in this for the punching, the hitting and the lashing out wasn't the way to do it.

'I want to get stronger,' I said. It was still the truth.

He held up a pad for me and asked me to hit it. I could only come up with a light, weedy thwack. Marc's arm barely moved.

He stepped back on the soft matted studio floor, got me to shift my weight slightly, told me to try again. He told me that in society we're conditioned to be soft, to hold back our physical power in case we hurt someone.

'Next time you punch, scream,' he said.

I looked at him blankly, but he nodded, so I took a deep breath.

'Waah,' I tried feebly, and he laughed, batting off another useless attack.

'You see, you're still holding back. I didn't say fake-scream, I said scream. Big breath – scream like Satan himself is coming after you. Don't worry about who can hear you – the music's too loud next door.'

'Waah . . .' *Thwack.*

Even more feeble.

It felt like a nightmare I'd been having for years – someone is chasing me, grabbing me, but when I try to push them away my arms are like rubber and when I hit out all the force is lost. I didn't want to be that person. I closed my eyes, didn't think about the pad or Marc, blocked out the pounding grime track from the other studio, the scent of stale sweat in the air, the dampness in the gloves. Instead I used that anger swirling in me. I drew it in, pushed it to the end of my fist and roared.

The pad moved – not much more, but it moved. Marc smiled, showing a row of white teeth and one gold one.

'Nice rage,' he said. 'Now we have to work on your discipline.'

And so I did. I trained like crazy for months, switching from one-on-one lessons to group, and learning to spar. I felt my body change, tighten up. I moved differently and when I was in the gym, I felt like a different person. The energy I felt pulsing through me might have been to do with exercise but there was more to it than that. There was discipline, focus and a purity of intention forming in my mind.

I had no idea whether Marc knew my history – if he did, he never let on. He never flinched or hesitated when he talked about 'an attacker coming at you' or 'your opponent'.

I loved that, too, the freedom to talk about punching someone as if it was OK to think about these things. The freedom to ask, 'Could I ever bring down a fully grown man on my own?'

Marc laughed and shook his head. 'Forget that *Marvel* movie bullshit,' he said. 'It just can't happen. It's not sexist – it's just physics. Men have more bulk to use against you and most of them are stronger. If you work on your grappling you'll stand more of a chance – but no, don't go getting into fights with men.'

I felt red-hot anger flow through me as I turned away. I stalked across the room to where a kid called Bradley was mucking about with his friends and just grappled him.

It took seconds to get him to the floor – Bradley surprised, weeping pitifully, his mates standing around in shock. I still had him pinned when Marc pulled me off him and I kept struggling, my limbs thrashing against Marc's rock-like muscles. He restrained me until I ran out of energy. It was only then that I looked up and saw the anger and disappointment in his face.

'Get out,' he said.

Pulling my fleece on, I ran out into the rain, Bradley's sobs and Marc's stony glare filling my mind. Tears of shame squeezing from my eyes. I wasn't seeing straight and charged right into a thin, angular woman standing under the bandstand.

I drew back, expecting cursing and more anger, but instead the woman said, 'God bless you.'

She looked at me with milky blue eyes. Her bony right hand was held over her heart, which lay beneath a sodden maroon anorak. Her left hand clutched, claw-tight, at a sheaf of flyers. 'God bless you, my child.'

Something glued me to the wet, shiny pavement in front of her. I didn't know what to say.

'Do you have Jesus in your life?' she asked.

Nobody had ever asked that before, and I felt oddly ashamed as I answered. 'No, not really.'

'You need to let Him in,' she said. 'Without Him, we are lost.'

Lost. It was like a sign, like she knew. She could see her words sinking in and her gaze was burning now – she had found someone.

'Nobody can help me,' I said. I wanted to explain that what I'd lost was so big, it was beyond mere miracles, but the truth was buried too deep inside me now. I couldn't let it out without a whole flood of toxic hatred coming with it. Instead I said: 'I just did something really bad.'

'Oh, child.' She shook her head and smiled, the smile of someone who really did feel she had the answers. I found my feet, started to walk away. I could feel the rain now, soaking into my trainers. I shivered in my sweaty gym gear.

'Wait,' she said. Her hand grabbed my arm and I panicked, nearly screamed. *No sudden movements,* Dad always told people. I pulled away. But then she shoved something into my hand, a book – *the* book.

'It's mine,' the woman said. 'It's brought me great comfort down the years, I hope it will do the same for you.'

I took it – I didn't know how to turn it down – and then I ran. I didn't say thank you. To this day I feel guilty about not saying thank you.

The book was small and ordinary looking and covered in a black plastic protective layer. Gold letters on the front informed me there was Good News inside. I tucked it inside my fleece against the rain and as I felt it through the thin material, my heart jumped. A small, square solution, the answer, the light.

Back home I nodded to Dad and scrambled up the stairs to the Hole, peeling out of my wet clothes and into dry pyjamas so I could read.

This bible was old. The woman, Anna, had written her name in it in fountain pen which had blurred with the rain. Passages were underlined, scraps of paper bearing shopping lists and the keys to the universe were tucked between the pages and, in Mark's Gospel, a pressed daisy. I opened it to a random page.

The Lord is merciful and will not reject us forever. He may bring us sorrow, but his love for us is sure and strong . . .

I read on, hungrily, for hours. My brain filled with the words, everything seemed to have meaning – as if it was talking directly to me. Inside me something started to loosen – feelings that had been clenched tight for years, throbbing endlessly through my head. Maybe, if God loved me, I wouldn't have to feel this way. I could just stop.

I sat up almost all night. I underlined beneath Anna's own lines. I folded down corners.

'Thank you, Anna,' I murmured to myself as I lay my head on the faded pattern of my pillowcase. And then, for the first time since I could remember, I prayed.

Belief took hold of me, and grew in me as the weeks passed, like the fire they describe in the Bible, or the seeds springing on fertile ground. Wherever I was – hiding in the cupboard at school or listening to a lecture from one of our volunteers – God was with me. I felt like He was actually sitting inside my head looking through my eyes.

But then I began thinking about sin.

I thought about all the lies I'd told. To Dad: *Yeah, of course I'm OK.* To the people who came to CAREY fundraisers: *I believe in forgiveness – and thanks for all the teddy bears, I love 'em!* To all those journalists who had asked their sensitively phrased questions: *I just want to move on. I don't think about the past.*

My deadliest sin, though, was anger. The rage which made me lash out at Bradley, which filled me every time I thought about Crow. My anger had let Crow in in the first place, it had started everything. I was as sinful and guilty as he was.

I tried to make amends, screwed up those vicious drawings and scribblings I'd made, shoved them into Kentucky's belly and sealed them in with one of Mum's old brooches. I wanted to burn that bear but I still couldn't bring myself to do it, so instead I prised the bottom off my wardrobe and sealed him inside, nailing the board back down with thumb tacks as I prayed.

Next, I went to Marc to say sorry and wrote an official letter of apology to Bradley. I told them I was working on my anger issues. I was banned for a month so I could think about what I'd done.

I didn't care. I didn't need to learn to fight now that I was learning to forgive.

*   *   *

The fire of faith burned in my brain for months. Sometimes it warmed me, gave me something to hold onto which was all mine – hope that somehow my sins would be forgiven. Other times, alone at night, it scorched me as I prayed for forgiveness and sobbed at how unworthy I was.

And then one day, the landline rang and I answered. I heard a nervous male voice at the end.

'Is this CAREY?'

My sister's name hit me in the guts like always and I stuttered out a no.

'You need the office number,' I said, reciting it from memory.

'OK, thanks. Is that . . . Leah?' The voice suddenly went tight and excited. 'It is, isn't it? I'm an intern at the *Daily News* and I was wondering what your thoughts were now that Crow has been moved to a cushy, low-security jail?'

Still reeling from Carey's name, hearing Crow's was like a double punch. I couldn't process it and sank down onto the old chair, the receiver slithering from my hands. Later the paper's editor would apologise to Dad for the intern's clumsy call, but the damage was done.

I tried to calm myself by reading the Bible, but the spell was broken. There was no thrill of faith and certainty any more. A cushy jail – comfortable and safe. No straw mattress, no rats gnawing his blankets at night. Prison had come a long way since *The Count of Monte Cristo*.

I kept reading my bible, kept trying. I went back over my underlining and Anna's underlining, willing that magical feeling to come back. But other phrases pulled at my attention now. Eyes for eyes, teeth for teeth.

Any who commit murder shall be put to death . . .

A life for a life . . .

And then this last one:

Human beings were made like God, so whoever murders one of them will be killed by someone else.

I took my pen, underlined it three times and wrote in the margin, in big, rounded thirteen-year-old handwriting:

CROW

The next day I was back at MMA. *Punch, kick, punch . . .* I made sure to avoid Bradley's eye, making nice for Marc. The fever of religion had faded, but I knew one thing for certain now – Marc was wrong. I could do this. My anger was a good thing, giving me the strength I needed to make things right again.

A life for a life.

Chapter 13

Boyd, before

He's out.

I saw him, the old bastard, clear as day, sitting on a bench outside the Rose. His leathery old face crinkled into a thousand death-grey folds as his eyes squinted in the morning sunlight. He's not used to the sun any more.

The others are seething in my mind – raging at him and at me. Telling me the same thing they said when they first roared into my head after Kyle had gone.

You're bigger, you're stronger – you could have stopped him.

You should have taken a knife and stuck it in his gut.

You should have ended him before it happened.

They listed the million chances when I could have intervened – the time Tony went for Kyle in the kitchen and I thought about throwing myself between them but didn't. The time Kyle made too much noise during the football and I could have taken him out to the park or something, but I stayed put because I wanted to see the match. The time I snivelled in our room while Tony grabbed him by the throat and pinned him against a wall.

Eight years old.

Eight fucking miserable years.

The doctors said Tony had nothing to do with what happened. That kids are vulnerable to meningitis – that parents miss the symptoms; they think it's just the flu. But Kyle was tired, and when I scooped him up into the ambulance his little arms and legs felt skinny, delicate and trembling like a bird's bones. This was a kid with all the fight gone out of him, no strength left for battling off infections. There's only so much doctors can do.

After the hospital and all the sad form-filling and pointless paperwork, Mum lost it. Tony lost it. I just hid under Kyle's Iron Man duvet, crushing his pillow over my ears with clammy hands, while they fought it out. I didn't even care which of them was left standing at the end.

That's when the others started to show up. Troy arrived first, with his sarcasm, his poison. Soon after came Bart, his foul-mouthed and filthy-minded sidekick. I can't even remember when Frankie showed up – he just sort of sidled in later, as if I'd left the back door in my brain open. More voices rustled in the background, still weak but getting stronger.

Weed helped calm things – until it didn't. Until the others were with me 24/7, pushing and sniping, jostling for control.

But I never did anything to Tony. Six weeks after Kyle's death he got in a fight in a pub and got sent down. So the cops ended up doing my job for me, taking him from us.

They told Mum he was going away for a long time. They lied.

Now here he is, pint in hand, fingers drumming impatiently on the wooden table in front of him. He's restless. In a minute he'll be up, back to his dad's. But he'll soon get bored there and start looking for a soft touch with a cosy flat. He'll be knocking on Mum's door.

I've changed since last time – the Crew has taught me things. Now I know how to bring a man down, how to really hurt someone.

All the fights I've had, every punch and kick – now I realise they were just practice for Tony.

'We need a knife,' Troy said.

The one I've been carrying in my pocket for years is shit – a small kitchen knife reinforced with duct tape which makes it easier to grip and hides the fact that Mum used to use it for slicing potatoes. I keep it sharp, but it's not really going to scare anybody.

When it comes to choosing a new one, I step aside and let Frankie take over. He's the quietest of the others, but he's the one with an eye for detail. Whenever I fuck up, Troy and Bart will laugh and call me names, but Frankie is the one who spends hours analysing, point by point, exactly what I've done wrong. So he does all the online research about the ideal weight, the best grip, the easiest one to conceal. He finds somewhere that will sell it to me.

It's in my hands within a few days, and I love it. Shiny steel with a wicked, jagged edge. It's heavy in my pocket, makes me feel important, strong.

Sometimes having voices in my head is like having a crew all of my own. I thank Frankie politely.

'Now you've got no excuses, you snivelling little roid on the arsehole of humanity,' says Frankie. 'Do it. End him. A life for a life.'

Chapter 14

Leah, sixteen

Crowds of people were jostling at me. An elbow in my back, an isotonic drink spilled over my shoes leaving a sticky yellow stain. All around me people crying and hugging and clapping their hands. I'd joined in at first but then my hands got sore and so were my feet. A CAREY volunteer was fluttering around me, rearranging my hair into that Pollyanna style Dad always insisted on when we went out in public – the top bit pulled back off my face and fastened with a ribbon like I was a child on her first day at school and not a sixteen-year-old girl. I swayed slightly with fatigue.

'Shall we sit down on the grass for a while?' the volunteer said.

I shook my head. This volunteer was newish, and I was still in the process of educating her, the same way I'd taught all the others. *I'm not an invalid. Something completely shitty happened to me nine years ago but I'm perfectly capable of standing.* I checked she wasn't looking and discreetly lifted one foot to give it a rest.

I've never understood why people want to do the London Marathon. Nobody is really designed to run that far. It messes with your heart, your lungs, your digestive system.

People actually soil themselves on the way round – did you know that? There has to be a better way to raise money. Over the past six months I'd seen Dad limping home from training sessions, soaked by the rain, chafed by the freezing air, nearly crying as he lowered his stiff, tired body down onto the sofa. I'd seen him get thinner and wirier, he moved differently, and he thought differently, too. He still talked about George Eliot and Thomas Hardy, but he also started quoting soppy inspirational phrases like: 'Don't stop when you're tired – stop when you're done,' or 'When your legs can't run any more, run with your heart.' His breakfast chats were peppered with runner-speak, words like 'tapering' and 'carb loading'. He checked his Just Giving page about thirty times a day, making sure that the CAREY Twitter feed gave a shout of thanks every time some Christian granny donated a tenner to the cause.

'You will be there at the end for me, won't you?' he asked.

I promised, and so here I was, accompanied by this blonde volunteer who seemed to think I was going to have a panic attack any second, and was probably disappointed that it hadn't happened yet.

That was the thing which drove me mad about the volunteers – they wanted me to be weak, they wanted me to fall down so they could help pick me up. This new one was the worst – she kept asking me stupid questions like 'What's your favourite band?' and 'Do you like pizza?' And then there was the classic: 'I have a daughter about your age – you should meet her, I'm sure you'd get on.'

Yes, because being the same age is all you need to have in common, right? That's why schools are such happy places, full of children skipping around hand-in-hand in perfect harmony.

I felt exposed here, vulnerable. Around me on the lawns of St James's Park strangers were chatting and making friends, talking about which loved one was running the marathon and why.

My Eric's been doing it for years, slowly but surely like a tortoise . . . It's Emma's first go – she's doing it for Mencap . . . I did it last year and I'd LOVE to do it again but, you know, injuries . . .

I kept my eyes slightly glazed over – if I avoided eye contact, nobody would try chatting to me, or start asking me the questions they warn you about in the CAREY guidelines. I knew I looked aloof and snobbish but I just couldn't keep my public face on for this long.

The volunteer was looking more and more distracted. Every time a new runner staggered into sight her eyes darted towards them. Her hands fluttered and fussed around her hair, pushing a strand behind one ear, pulling it forward again, pushing it back. Then her fingers started to tweak at the zip of her pink fleece – up a bit, down a bit . . .

'I thought he'd be finished by now,' she said. 'He thought he'd do it in under five hours. He said he'd be all right but what if it's too much? What if he's injured somewhere along the way?' This was new – normally volunteers never said anything which might make me afraid. A strange sensation crept over me as I realised she wanted *me* to say something reassuring. But before I could pull a sentence together she was crying out in relief. 'Oh! Oh thank God!'

I followed her gaze, saw Dad limping towards us, sweat dripping from his hair, his nose. There was a smear of blood at nipple-level on his soaking wet CAREY T-shirt, a dazed, blank look on his face and a tinfoil blanket around his shoulders.

Then before I could take a step forward, the volunteer surged in front of me and threw her arms out and around my father. 'Oh David, oh well done, you're amazing!'

Dad kind of leaned into her, his legs buckling. His arms flapped helplessly at his sides for a few frantic seconds then folded her into a sodden, squishy hug. And he didn't let go.

What was this?

I stepped forward, and Dad loosened his grip on the volunteer, stretched out an arm and dragged me in. Now I was supporting him on one side, the volunteer on the other – a wave of fresh-sweat smell wafted over me and I felt it soak into my T-shirt. Under my arm, Dad was trembling and I could feel his ribs heaving, his stick-like legs were barely holding him up. Behind his back, the volunteer's hand brushed mine and drew back sharply, apologetically. We both knew she had been invading my personal space, but what else had she been invading?

Dad and the volunteer. Dad and – ugh – the volunteer . . .

'Leah!' A familiar voice – the short photographer with the big voice and the smile had got older and plumper now. His spiky hair was sparser and touched with grey – I imagined a wife, twin girls waiting for him to come home from covering this safe

London Marathon gig. But that smile was still the same and it held my gaze as he lifted his camera. In my head I started piecing together the situation – *how had it happened? When? How long?* But the photographer's smile kept me focused, reminded me people were watching. I grinned back at him like an old friend, feeling the smile creep into my eyes. People who say you can't fake a smile in your eyes are lying. *Flash, flash, flash* . . .

'Dad, I'm so proud of you,' I said, loudly enough for the journalists to hear. 'But please never do this again!'

They loved that one.

'Is this something you do all the time, then? Do you snog all the helpers?' I couldn't keep the hurt out of my voice.

I'd kept my happy face on for the cameras, and somehow stayed calm afterwards when he, Claire and I awkwardly sipped coffees among the other runners and families in the Waterstones café near Charing Cross. But with each passing hour a strange sense of hurt throbbed in my head, and once we were home I exploded.

Every day I wore the right clothes, styled my hair in the same perfect way, talked about the books I was reading, accepted teddy bear gifts with smiling grace, always hiding the real me to stop him worrying. It was my duty to be his girl, never to change, and he was Dad, forever mine. That was the deal. I'd always thought I would be the one to break it.

Dad's eyes looked back at me from two tired hollows, and I saw a flash of weariness beyond his post-Marathon drain. He took a deep, ragged breath.

'I didn't want you to find out this way.' he said.'I just didn't know how to tell you I'd met someone.'

I felt sick, like something had been scooped out of the middle of my body, leaving a big wet gap there. I listened to him go on about how funny Claire was, and how she was different from the other helpers. How they'd got chatting when they were working late during the Great Pre-Christmas Mailout Push last year, how much she cared, how much she listened.

'She's got a daughter your age. She's nice. A bit showy, but nice – you'll like her.'

A flash of rage.

'So *her* daughter knows? *Her* daughter's met you?'

His face collapsed into a look of horror as he realised what he'd said. I didn't speak, couldn't look at him any more. I whirled on the ball of my foot and swept out of the room. I didn't stop until I got to the Hole.

Huddled under the duvet, I screamed into the pillow, let myself thrash around, slammed my fists into the mattress – just five seconds of pure anger. This was my fault, I told myself. Everything changes, everyone goes away in the end – nothing will last. Why did I think Dad would be any different? Soon even the shop would crumble away beneath me and I'd have to start again with nothing.

Toughen up.

It was my own stupid fault for being so soft and relying on Dad not to let me down. How could I do what needed to be done if I was this weak?

*   *   *

That night, sleep wouldn't come. *He* appeared instead. Lying in his jail cell messing with my head the same way I tried to mess with his.

Everyone else has forgotten, he said. *Why don't you just let it go? Take a chill pill, date boys, put on some make-up, be a fucking girl.*

Oh you'd like that, wouldn't you? I threw back at him, into the darkness. *But one of us has to remember. You've changed, with all your reading and writing and getting clean when you should be a crumpled ball of regret howling in the night. Dad's changed – he laughs now. He's heard of people like Taylor Swift. He's working his way through Jamie Oliver's cookbooks. He pretends he still thinks about Mum and Carey but I bet he's forgotten Mum's face, her collection of scarves, or that time when Carey decided to change her name to George and wouldn't answer to anything else for weeks. He's started to believe the charity crap can fix him somehow. He's started to let go.*

I was the only one left, the only one who wanted to remember, and it weighed hard on my chest as I lay there, crushing the air out of my lungs. Somebody had to do something – it was only right that it should be me, the one who started it all.

I knew it lay in my power to give up and move on, just like Dad. But he'd still be out there, that thing we did together would still be burning away. I didn't deserve to rest until I'd done what was necessary. So letting go wasn't an option. The next day, I ordered the knife.

It took a lot of internet searching to find it – I had to borrow Dad's passport and order it in his name and then look out for it among the dozens of boxes of books that arrived every week.

'Nice to see you taking an interest in deliveries,' Dad said, as we rummaged through the post. Luckily I got to the small, compact parcel before he did, hiding it in the junk under the counter until he was distracted by his cataloguing. I didn't open it until later that night, when I was sure he was asleep.

And there it was. The same style that *he* used. A six-inch serrated hunting knife with a green handle and convenient silicone grips so your hand doesn't slip while you're stabbing. This was the knife I had seen in his hand, the one that had appeared in all the newspapers during the trial. It was a wicked, killing blade, purpose-built for cutting people. The prosecution had argued that nobody could possibly carry this knife without intending to use it on another human being.

The weight of it felt nice in my hand, there was a sense of power there and I could understand why it made people feel secure. But the blade – I couldn't shake the feeling that the blade had a mind of its own, that it would somehow find a way to turn on me and slice me if I didn't hold it firmly enough.

I wrapped it carefully and respectfully in an old cotton T-shirt before burying it deep in the case next to my bed. But that night, as I dropped off to sleep, I could still feel it there, pushing on the edge of my consciousness, trying to find a way to my heart.

Chapter 15

Ellie

It didn't matter how many plug-in air fresheners Mum put in Dylan's room – it still smelled like Boy: sheets that haven't been changed for months, damp washing, dust and Lynx. Biscuit crumbs and plastic debris peppered the rough grey carpet under my bare feet as I perched on the end of his bed, games controller in my hand.

Yes, I was hiding in Dylan's room playing *Hail of Bullets* like the complete and utter loser I was. I had no friends – they all thought I was some kind of paranoid drama queen. My mum was out sampling food at the wedding caterers with her fiancé, a man who disapproved of everything I did. And when they weren't around Leah had taken to staring at me with that ocean-deep blue gaze of hers, steady and calculating, like she was working out the best way to have me killed.

There was only one beacon of hope mixed in all this – the message I'd opened when I got home from school that day. It was only from Maxine bloody F. Yes, *the* MaxineF – she of the hilarious Star Wars Disney Princess lockdown mashup video that had basically taken over the internet for about a week last summer.

Loving your stepfamily posts. I can really relate! I've got an idea – bit out of the blue I know but shall we collab?

Even now, the thought of it made my hand tense up for a second on the trigger button making me accidentally kill another pensioner.

This collaboration could make our channel big, it could actually make DBLG into the success we'd always wanted it to be – hell, we could even start earning money from it. But instead of replying straight away I'd shut the laptop and fled – my heart beating with wild fight-or-flight panic.

Say yes and I could get everything I wanted.

Say yes and thousands more people would see the channel.

And those thousands of people could show their parents, who could show other parents, who could show *my* parents. I could already hear Mum and David's angry words in my head, the endless lectures, the scorn. Typical stupid Ellie, such an attention seeker she'd sell her own traumatised stepsister to go viral.

That's what they thought of me, and maybe that's all I was, really. A desperate wannabe with no talent, no real plans. The sort of loser you can smell a mile away when they show up on a TV reality show, begging 'look at me'.

But what if I ignored her? I'd never get a chance like this again, and I might even piss her off.

Ohgodohgodohgod.

'Come on, Ellie, you're not even trying,' Dylan shouted as my character went down in a storm of scarlet pixels. He gave me another lecture about the responsiveness of the software and how I had to lean into it and go with my instincts like a

Jedi. He'd just miraculously brought me back to life when there was a tap at the door.

'Come in, Leah,' Dylan said. A knot tightened in my chest. What was she doing knocking on Dylan's door, and why was he acting like it was something which happened a lot?

She peeked shyly around the door frame, saw me and drew back a little. 'I hope I'm not disturbing.'

'Um . . . we're not supposed to be playing this game,' Dylan said, looking downwards so that his un-gelled fringe flopped down over one eye. The action on screen had been paused just as Dylan's muscle-bound meathead of a character had opened fire into a queue at a virtual soup kitchen. It was about as violent as you could get.

Leah sidled into his room and pushed the door closed behind her. She smiled a slow, easy smile. 'You know,' she said, 'I'm really not as delicate as all that. It's only computer-generated blood.'

'I dunno, maybe you shouldn't . . .' I began.

'I'm a grown woman,' she snapped back. 'For God's sake, I'm not some sort of delicate flower.' She strode forward and held her hand out to me. Weakly, I passed her the controller I'd been holding. I couldn't speak, couldn't look at her. Since she had invaded my room, I had avoided her as much as I could and Leah had taken delight in making me uncomfortable. At mealtimes she would fix me with that even, calm stare, thanking me elaborately when I passed the salt and making conversation by asking the kind of question only parents usually ask, like, 'how's school?'

It was becoming harder and harder for me to play it cool.

But it seemed like all the while she and Dylan had been getting closer. I could tell by the easy, friendly way Dylan explained the rules and showed her the keys for up, down, jump, kick, punch and rapid fire. My brother seemed confident, almost grown-up as he let her into his own personal world. *When had this happened?*

She sat down next to him, her ankles kicking at the sides of the cabin bed, back straining forward to look at the screen. 'Prepare to be annihilated,' she said.

For the first five minutes she was just as useless as me, but then she started to get it. Run, jump, rapid fire, punch, kick . . .

'Score!' she laughed. On the screen her hapless victim crumpled to his knees. She emptied a few more rounds into him for good measure, until Dylan told her off for wasting ammo.

And again – kick, punch, jump, rapid fire . . . Another bad guy folded like a deck of cards. And again. And again.

I craned forward and stole a look at her face – her eyes were gleaming, face intent, staring at the screen. Her fingers and thumbs moved over the buttons like she was playing a musical instrument. She was in a state of bliss.

'Die, scum!' she said. Then she burst out laughing, the first genuine laugh I think I'd ever heard from her. It sounded kind of . . . free.

Dylan joined in the trash talk, and soon they were both firing away, snarling at the screen, locked into another world together. I fidgeted, flipping through some of Dylan's *X-Men* back issues, rearranging the collection of old water glasses on his bedside, but I could have been anywhere. Those two were in a bloodthirsty, shoot-em-up world of their own.

The livelier and more relaxed Leah seemed, the louder the laughter and the more points she racked up, the more cold and uneasy I felt. No video games, no TV, no scenes of violence, however pantomime or fake, must enter the house – David's rule had been clear. I'd always sneered at that, the idea that protecting Leah from the modern world would somehow keep her safe. But maybe he wasn't afraid of upsetting her – perhaps he was afraid of something else.

I don't think either of them saw me pad to the door and slip out, back to my own bedroom. I lay back on the bed, duvet cold and fresh against my cheek, staring up at Keiran's love-and-peace mural and reminding myself that I was the troublesome, disruptive one. My computer lay next to me where I'd left it, covered in childish glittery stickers, its green light blinking to indicate it was still on.

I took another look at that message and, despite everything, a bubble of happiness welled up inside. I shouldn't do the collab – I knew that. But this was EVERYTHING I'D EVER WANTED. And what else did I have?

I wasn't doing any harm, wasn't giving away any big family secrets, I was just being me. And now a really big online star had noticed me – and it was me she wanted, not Billie or Gloria.

So yes. I was going to do the collab. And yes, I did feel guilty about it. But it was the right thing to do – for me, for a change.

Chapter 16

Leah, present day

I'm looking at the knife again, tilting the blade, seeing my eyes reflected in it and trying to focus, to remember who I am and what I want to do. I need to be tough – to build on it every day. I suppose that's why psychopaths practise on animals before the big event, but unfortunately I'm not a psychopath. This would be a whole lot easier if I was. Instead I feel jelly-like, feeble and confused. I'm losing my focus and this new family is making it worse.

Dylan is bad enough – the way he accepts me and all my weirdness without question. He honestly doesn't care what I do or how I look provided I share his interests. I even let slip about my MMA skills the other day and he forced me to show him a bunch of moves he could use against the school bullies.

I don't want to be a sister again. I can't face it.

As for Ellie, she's a mystery. One day she acts like she wants to be friends, but then the next she's jumping at my shadow and snooping through my things. She's loud, dramatic and so full on that sometimes, after half an hour in the same room with her, I realise my jaw aches from grinding my teeth. But then she comes out with something so ridiculously funny I have to grind them harder to stop myself laughing.

The thing is, I think she's got some kind of secret, too. Sneakiness comes about as naturally to Ellie as transcendental meditation. She is one of life's sharers and yet over the past few weeks she's spent more and more time shut up in that room of hers. Yesterday I bumped into her as she scuttled along the hallway in her fluffy pink dressing gown, phone in hand gazing at whatever riveting Insta-tube-TikTok-snapcrappery was going on that day. She looked up at me and jumped so much her phone slithered out of her grasp, landing with a hard clatter on the thin rug. She dived for it quickly, cradling it like a puppy and shielding it against her chest while she looked up at me with an expression in her eyes . . . I think it might have been guilt.

It can't still be about that boy – he was clearly completely uninterested in her and her ego won't let her dwell on heartbreak for that long. It might be useful to find out what it is, but am I just distracting myself, procrastinating? The truth is, I've been drifting away from the Plan for a long while, and it all started with Thorpe Park.

Back then I was still hoping that the thing with Claire would pass, but even then part of me knew I was ignoring the signs. Mum's photograph, the faded one in the silver frame, had moved from Dad's bedside to the dresser in the hallway. Not gone, but no longer the last face he saw before he went to sleep at night. He had started coming out with things – snippets of knowledge that he'd never normally be interested in. Did I know that Beyoncé contributed to over thirty charities? Or that it was best to make béchamel with a whisk rather than stirring it with a fork? No, I didn't. In fact, up until then he'd called it cheese sauce and bought it in a jar.

He had even bought an Adele CD and talked about her powerful voice and raw songwriting talent as though it was the most normal thing in the world for him to do. Claire was putting down roots in our life, little ones at first, pushing through the soil and gripping on tight like a weed – harder and harder to pull out.

Sometimes I would come home from school to find her there, perched primly at the kitchen table nursing a mug of tea and flashing me a nervous please-like-me smile. On other days, Dad would kiss me lightly on the forehead before heading out for the evening with some stomach-churning joke about not waiting up. I'd spend the evening alone with the books and the quiet, wondering whether it was too late to take on the teenager's role in our household. Maybe that was what had gone wrong – one of us had to rebel and he had got tired of waiting for me.

He would return late, fumbling hastily through the shop in the half-drunk belief that he was sneaking past me.

It seemed like I was the only person who could see the monstrous wrongness of it. He was pretending to be someone else, aping normality to convince Claire we were a good prospect. It was unfair on her, on him and on me. Why was he bothering? It was only going to lead to even more hurt and loss, and she wasn't even that special.

Give me time, I wanted to tell him. *And I'll disappoint you plenty. You don't need to do this.*

And then he sprang it on me. A family bonding trip to Thorpe Park. In broad daylight, in public, finally meeting Ellie and Dylan.

'It seems like a fun way to break the ice,' Dad said. At least it might have been him speaking. Dad's lips were moving, but it was Claire's voice that I heard.

I wanted to shake him, yell at him. We didn't do theme parks, in the same way we didn't do Netflix or Facebook or any other useless wastes of time. What was he thinking? But now wasn't the time to lose control, and that's how I found myself strapped like a toddler into the back seat of Claire's battered estate car, fighting the urge to ask *are we there yet?*

Nothing – not Dad's fakery or Claire's vapid factoids – had prepared me for my first real exposure to Planet Ellie.

I mean, I know girls. I go to an all-girls school and watch them feed off each other, each pretending to be so individual while desperately trying to be the same. The stench of make-up and body spray and the scrum in front of the sixth-form toilet mirrors at home time. The phones thrown back and forth through the class so a Snapchat post or Instagram exchange could be analysed by the widest spread of people.

I never talk to them. I keep my head down. I don't meet their eyes and they've been ignoring me for years now. But Ellie is something different. She's like the essence of girls magnified, multiplied, girls on steroids. Every time she walked into a room it was like an invisible band played *ta-DAH*!

She talked non-stop in the car on the way down – wittering on about school stage productions, make-up contouring

135

techniques, this or that reality show person, and who was endorsing various products. She talked about bands, boys, films, online stuff I'd never even heard of. For twenty minutes on the way down she'd played me video clips of someone called MaxineF showing us what she'd got for her birthday.

'It's funny because Maxine's got this thing about leopard-print and – see, she was given six leopard scarves,' she'd told me.

I'd wanted to say that if you have to explain why something is funny then it's definitely not funny, but I let my silence do the talking. Eventually she left me alone and started arguing with her brother about whether his hairy horrible leg had invaded her sovereign territory.

I thought about Carey, bound tightly up in her kiddy car seat, so carefully and safely strapped in by Mum and how, even though she could barely move, she still found ways of spreading her things into my half of the car. She had accumulated bits of plastic – spiky toy dinosaurs; princesses of different shapes and sizes; cars; miniature ponies, some with real flowing manes and tails. Everywhere she went there had been a trail of pink, shiny, made-in-China tat.

She would be just like Ellie by now, trying to daub her nails with sparkly varnish in a moving vehicle, while kicking her sibling with one foot. Funny, popular, full of life and energy.

Then I thought of her legs, motionless and stiff, that little blue shoe . . .

A sick twist of pain in my belly, before I turned off the thought in the usual way by thinking of him, far away in prison, safe from me, for now.

The theme park was just as I expected – stuff in your face all the time. Jangling music, clanking machinery and in the background, the rising and falling rhythm of children's screams. Kids pushing past and fat parents sailing after them like human landslides, laden down with chips, burgers and vats of cola. There were teenagers in packs – the girls all midriff and pouting selfies, pretending to have the best time ever; the boys with their shoulders hunched, shuffling along, pretending not to care about anything.

Ellie and Dylan surged ahead, making a beeline for the largest, scariest roller coaster. One where your feet dangle from your chair as you swoop around the rails. I joined the end of the queue without even thinking about it.

Dad hadn't been able to hide his shock. Was I sure? I didn't have to do this, just because Ellie was. Ellie's eyes flickered over to us – I knew she'd heard, and I felt my cheeks go hot with anger and shame.

Was this my role? Was I supposed to come to a theme park and not go on any of the rides?

Then my auto-smile kicked in. I hugged Dad and told him I'd be fine, that it couldn't be that bad, could it? I threw in a little comedy grimace which made him relax.

And that is how, after an agonised hour of queuing (enduring Ellie's monologue, A History Of YouTubers Who Have Been To Thorpe Park) I was sliding into a hard plastic seat, which swayed slightly as I climbed into it. I stared straight ahead as Ellie wriggled into the one next to me, fidgeting with excitement.

'Watch out for that first loop,' she said. 'It's pretty extreme.'

I clamped my jaw tight shut at her friendly tone, and her glib assumption that I'd never been on a roller coaster before. Which I hadn't.

When we were all aboard, someone must have flipped a switch somewhere as a black vice-like mechanical arm clamped itself down hard over my shoulders. I couldn't escape.

Instinctively I tensed, thrashed, my breath became tight and panicky – only my awareness of Ellie's gaze kept me in control. Without her I would have screamed and screamed to be let off. I talked myself down. I was better than this. If I couldn't take this, how could I possibly endure what was to come? *This is just another test.*

I dug my fingernails into the crash barrier, stuck the smile back in place and fixed my eyes ahead.

Slowly, jerkily we began to move forward. A gentle lift, the breeze on my face, damp with drizzle as we climbed slowly up. Somewhere at the back a girl was screaming already, escalating little yips of anticipation that filled me with contempt. I glanced at Ellie and she rolled her eyes in agreement.

We went around the first curve – my legs flew outwards, the shoulder clamp chafed, and I felt a gentle pull on my shoes as we rounded a bend into a tunnel and out again. The screamer kicked up a notch and Ellie gave a derisive little snort of laughter.

Slowly we crept uphill, the machinery creaking and clanking alarmingly – which made me grateful that Dad was down on the ground as I could do without him worrying. I could see him and Claire – two doll-like figures with their arms around each other, Dad's eyes searching me out. I raised my hand to wave, but it never happened as we spun into the first loop which very nearly ripped my face off.

Faster, harder, round, up, down. I was floating, then crashing, then floating again in the space of a few moments. A strange feeling was bubbling inside me, something completely out of control that I couldn't even describe. It must have been less than two minutes before we were screeching to a halt at the end of the line and I realised what that strange sensation was.

I was laughing.

'We are definitely doing that again,' said Ellie.

Back on land, my legs wove and wobbled, the bubbles of laughter kept coming up inside me and my pulse continued to race. Ellie took a picture of herself, me reeling in the background, Dylan strutting about pretending the ride hadn't affected him at all, but looking a bit green around the mouth.

'I'm going to put it on Snapchat,' Ellie explained.

I asked her why – why would people possibly want to see a photo of us staggering about in front of a cheerily painted theme park bin?

'Hey, not everything's going to go viral,' she said. 'But you have to keep uploading content – so people get to know you.'

I felt like two-year-old Carey then, during that phase when she would answer any question or request with a whiny 'But *whyyyyyy*?'

Why is it important to build your content and let people get to know you? It wasn't like she had a message to get out there beyond: *This Is Me, Ellie – Ta-DAH!*

Before I could form the question, Ellie was off through the crowd, heading for the next-most-terrifying roller coaster. I began to thread my way after her, wondering if the payoff of the ride was worth the hour of the wait.

Later, there were burgers and shakes in a plastic-fantastic restaurant – Dad discussing the environmental impact of takeaway packaging, Claire very efficiently ripping her empty drinks cup until it became a jagged little crown. She put it on her head and looked to one side. Dad burbled with laughter.

I could see them exchanging little looks every now and then. Tiny bubbles of hope. *It's going well, isn't it? Maybe this will work after all . . .*

By about 4 p.m., though, something changed. Dad yanked Claire to one side, hissing something into her ear. Claire looked flustered, defensive and guilty. Ellie was all wounded dignity, her lower lip jutting out by a mile. Dylan, I noticed, had all the emotional empathy of a brick and I liked him for it – he was the only person there not tripping up over everyone else's feelings. We went for ice cream, and then home.

Opening the door to the shop, smelling that rush of musty air, felt like a warm comfort blanket. I knew Dad wanted tea and feedback in the kitchen, but just this once I fell out of line and creaked my way up the steps to the Hole. I needed to be somewhere still and quiet, away from anyone's voices. I could tell Dad was about to argue, but then his phone rang.

I assumed it was Claire calling for a post mortem, but he answered in his official CAREY voice – all decisive and manly and not at all like the real him, and after a couple of moments listening he started to climb the stairs to the flat, keeping his voice calm all the while. 'Mmm-hmm, yes, one moment please . . .'

My nerves were jangling, but I was too tired to follow and eavesdrop.

I should have done, though. It would have saved me the squirming agony of Dad's carefully composed chat the next morning – a hypocritical monologue all about forgiveness and moving on. It would have given me time to prepare, to get my head round another new reality – because that was our Victim Liaison Officer, calling to tell us that Crow had been scheduled for release.

Two weeks later, Crow stepped out of the front gates of his prison and into a new town, a new home, and even a new identity, thanks to all the media attention his trial had received. I pictured him blinking in the sunlight like the Count of Monte Cristo, a shabby rucksack over his back, walking slowly towards his future on wobbly legs. I should have been waiting right there and done the deed straight away, but nobody was kind enough to tell me the exact time

– perhaps it was government policy to stop victims ambushing their attackers, or perhaps Dad knew and pretended not to. Instead, Crow just disappeared.

The media was almost as enraged as I was – furious he'd been allowed to go free and that he'd been protected from their righteous justice with a new identity and – no doubt – a nice council house and other luxuries at the taxpayer's expense.

Here is the press release that CAREY sent out as the story became public:

> For the past nine years CAREY has been tireless in its quest to ensure that what happened to Jane and Carey Stoke should not happen to anyone else. Boyd White's personal history was part of the inspiration behind our charity's beginnings but since then we have raised millions and helped thousands of disadvantaged young people. The cause has become much bigger than one case. We believe wholeheartedly in redemption, restorative justice and in prison as a route to rehabilitation rather than punishment. If an offender shows signs of reform and readiness to re-enter the world, to the satisfaction of the experts who work within the penal system, then we wholeheartedly support his or her release.

What a bunch of balls.

I wondered what had happened to the righteous, raging Dad I'd glimpsed all those years ago in the shop. Had Claire cured him of his hatred? Had it just been squashed out of him by logic, decency and the charity's relentless love-and-peace message?

Or maybe he was like me, just waiting to explode.

Whatever the reality, Dad's nails were chewed to stubs and he started on the skin around them, peeling off little slivers when he didn't think I was looking. Claire's face became pinched and strained when she looked at him. Both of them studied me intensely, looking for signs I was going to crack. I didn't give them the satisfaction.

And then – out of nowhere – Dad proposed to Claire. I guess that's one way of saying fuck you to an enemy, but maybe not the most romantic way of sealing a relationship.

So the wedding plans began, and we find ourselves here, listening to each other's grumbles and snores at night, sitting around the dinner table playing with our food and loading the dishwasher without talking. We're trying to squash our families together and pretend that Dad and Claire's love – if it really is love – can somehow shape the rest of us into one group-hugging whole.

I know what I should be doing. I should be tracking down Crow, making preparations, but I don't even know how to begin. Online, the news reports just say 'seaside town', which is no help at all. I'm not a private detective or a journalist (although all the newspapers seem to already know where Crow is living and are desperate to reveal it). I'm just a girl who lives behind an old bookshelf in a shop.

So I wait, I carry on with my fake part – venting some of my anger on Dylan's pixelated enemies or sparring in the gym – and playing fascinating mind games with Ellie. Ellie, the unrelentingly public personality who has a secret.

A secret.

I laugh. The most bleeding ridiculously obvious idea has just occurred to me. I am deeply ashamed I never thought of it before.

I google her.

Chapter 17

Ellie

There was something about her face at breakfast that struck me with stone-cold horror. She wasn't doing anything different – just eating her cereal in that neat little way of hers, ignoring the hideous family interlopers around her. But as I sat down in my usual spot, her eyes flickered up and met mine for a split second. The left corner of her mouth twitched into a slight smile. A look that said: *I've got you.*

Panic swept through me based on that look alone. I didn't need any more information than that – all I wanted to do was squirm out of her laser gaze. My first instinct was to drown it out – I turned to Mum and just started talking, an endless tide of waffle about bridesmaids' hairstyles, and how Leah and I should both get a lilac dip dye to match the dresses (ha ha!), and that I'd seen this amazing thing on Instagram about it last week. I filled the air with chatter, squeezing out anyone else's chance to speak – all the while keeping half an eye on Leah as she crunched her muesli. Waiting for her intake of breath, the sly, knowing comment that would follow. I didn't know what she was planning, just that something had shifted, that she had something she wanted to tell me and that she was mightily smug about it.

As I prattled on, my brain disengaged and I planned my exit. If I could get out of the house – as far as the bus to school, I'd escape somehow. Perhaps Leah would forget whatever dig she wanted to make and move on.

'Anyway, I'm late, got to run!' Peck Mum's cheek, punch Dylan lightly on the shoulder, grab bag . . . scarper.

Slamming the flimsy shop door behind me, I speed-walked down the street, past the boarded-up DVD rental, past the three different e-cig vaping lounges, the betting shop, the charity shop. My calf muscles started to ache under the strain, but I kept walking, occasionally bursting into an undignified trot. I was sweating in my school coat, my hair tangled hopelessly with my tie and my bag strap and strangling me. I realised I'd forgotten my phone and my theatre studies homework but there was no way I was going back now.

Safely round the corner I leaned back against a fence, breathed in the rich, creosote scent and tried to calm down. Hands shaking, I rummaged in the depths of my bag until I found a crumpled pack of cigarettes and lit one.

I was one of those smoke-the-odd-one-while-drunk people – I just happened to have Gloria's cigarettes on me – so after one big over-dramatic draw I was coughing my lungs out.

'You really are terrible at smoking,' Leah said.

I closed my eyes. Opened them again. Yes, she really was there, leaning against the fence with her arms crossed. I realised she must have ducked down the alleyway at the back of the shop, then jumped over the low wall at the back of the

DVD place, just to cut me off. She wasn't even out of breath. She reached out and took the cigarettes from me.

'Marlboro Lights, how unoriginal.' She took one, slid the lighter out of the packet and sparked it up, then took a perfect, elegant draw like a 1940s starlet. 'Want to know something else that's unoriginal? Your camera work. Sloppy, static. No depth of field.'

Oh.

Ohhhh . . . A hot feeling swept over me, I felt sick. I thought of her sitting in her little cell, watching all those YouTube posts on her laptop. Me talking about the unspecified 'weirdness' I was struggling with, the post about the Stepfamily Timebomb, the *Draw My Life* I'd done where I'd sketched the shop as a Gothic Transylvanian castle with book-bats flapping around it. I wanted to scream at her that she'd been listening to my private thoughts – but how could I? I'd stuck it all online and watched excitedly as the number of views and likes went up.

'I haven't done anything wrong!' I said, but Leah was just looking at me and shaking her head, like I was some unruly kid who needed to be put on the naughty step. Leah, with her secret scrawlings and sneaky plans. The girl whose inner life I'd been protecting for *months*. Right then I forgot every time I'd ever felt sorry for her, everything she'd ever been through – all I wanted to do was punch her in that glowing-skinned, self-satisfied face of hers.

I couldn't. I couldn't. Mum was going to be mad enough with me as it was. I took an angry pull on the cigarette again, held the coughing in, and clenched my other hand into a tight fist.

'Well I suppose someone was going to find it sooner or later,' I forced myself to say. 'Mum's going to go mad. Dave will throw me out for sure.'

Oh God. This might split them up.

Yes, these are things I should have thought of while I was making all those films. But it's easy – sitting there in your bedroom, just you and the camera. It's simple to be yourself, to drop all the pretences and imagine that your YouTube channel is actually a blank diary page. When I was making those vlogs – not the funny sketches or the beauty reviews but the real, honest talking ones – I felt like I was confiding something to my best friend.

A few times I'd thought they might see it. Or maybe that Dylan would see it, or one of Mum's friends' kids might, and word would get back to them. But every time that idea cropped up, my brain had just switched the thought off. I wanted to do this so badly I just couldn't picture it coming to an end, in the same way that it's impossible for someone to really imagine what it would be like to die. Well, for most of us, anyway.

She held her cigarette out in front of her, watching the smoke twist and curl around her fingers and away in the breeze. For a while she didn't speak, just watched it smoulder.

'I'm not going to tell,' she said. 'If you do something for me.'

If I hadn't been so terrified, I'd have burst out laughing. Was this girl serious, or auditioning for some bad gangster movie? 'What, do you want me to kill someone or something?'

Leah made a dry *hah* sound.

'No,' she said, smiling. 'I want you to talk to a photographer.'

So, it was because of Leah that Mum, Dylan and me got to go to the Amazing Children Awards. She and David had been going for years – either because she was nominated or, in the last couple of years, to present a bravery award to a younger kid, welcoming them into the shitty bad luck survivors' club. Dressing in black tie and hanging out with newspaper editors was David's idea of hell but he said it kept the charity in the public eye and that's what brought the donations in. Usually the invitation was Admit Two Only, but on the night after our friendly blackmail chat, Leah persuaded David to email the newspaper which organised it and request tickets for the rest of us too.

It would bring us closer as a family, Leah said.

By coincidence, it would also get me close to the photographer she wanted me to talk to. I had no idea what her plan was, but I think if she'd asked me to kill someone, I might have felt less uneasy about it. If Mum and David found out about the vlog, I'd be in trouble, but if they spotted me actually talking to a press photographer I might as well pack my bags and pick out a cardboard box down by the canal.

Part of me hoped that the paper's editor would turn us down flat. But who could resist the chance to get the inside scoop on Tragic David Stoke Finding Love Again and a peek inside the life of the weirdest stepfamily in Britain?

Ever since I could remember I'd wanted my name and picture in the papers – but not as Leah's bolt-on sister, thank you very much.

On the same day that David sent his email to the newspaper, I went online and took down all my DBLG posts. I didn't take down the comedy sketches, or the beauty and music stuff that I did with the others – I couldn't do that to Billie and Gloria, not when subscriptions were growing. But my stepfamily stuff had got the most views, the most likes. Back when I'd started the channel, that would have been enough for me. All I wanted to do was entertain, for people to know my name, look at my stuff and think, 'Yeah, I like her.' But as I took them down, it wasn't the lost fame that bothered me, it was the comments underneath from other people, struggling to fit in with a new parent, a new brother or sister. *This is exactly how I feel ... My mum wants to play happy families but it's just not real ... It feels like I'm the only earthling in a family of aliens ...*

Of course, there were a few trollish ones telling me to grow up and get a life, but most of them were so supportive. All I knew about them was the information I could squeeze out of their username and tiny profile pic, but I felt weirdly close to them. As I took each video down, I felt more alone than I'd been in a long time. Those people out there had understood me, made me feel less selfish, that what I was going through was natural.

And then I came to the collab with MaxineF and I was stuck. It was Maxine's post not mine – I had no control over it. I couldn't bear to email her and ask her to take it down. God, the embarrassment. I closed the lid of my laptop and tried not to think about it.

Meanwhile, the situation in the flat grew unbearable. I started eating breakfast in my room, unwilling to risk bumping into Leah. I couldn't shake the idea that she would come into my room again, go through my stuff. One night I even slept with a chair propped under my door handle, which led to a huge telling off from Mum when she tried to come in with a cup of tea the next morning.

I was hardly sleeping. I had bags under my eyes and spots around my mouth.

Mum, of course, didn't have a clue what was going on because Leah was being insanely friendly to me – complimenting my hairstyle, offering me a glossy book of *Vogue* covers from the shop, joining in the dinner-table conversation. And constantly asking me about vloggers.

'So, this Maxine leopard-print person – where would I find her channel?' she asked, all innocence, as we sat around chewing slowly on David's experimental risotto. 'Are there people who do book vlogs? They might be a bit more my thing.'

David and Mum exchanged a sickly, happy smile they thought we couldn't see. *Ah, so lovely to see the children playing together.*

Then Leah gave a sad little sigh and said something that didn't make sense to me: 'Oh yes, I forgot – my computer . . .'

Mum and David looked at each other again.

'Actually, I've been meaning to ask you something, Ellie,' Mum said. 'Leah's laptop has died, and we can't afford another one right now. I know you use your phone and iPad for pretty much everything, so would you mind sharing for a couple of months? Just for homework.'

Bloody Leah. She knew exactly what she was doing. After dinner I went back to my room and backed up all my photos and videos online, dragged everything else onto a memory stick, cleared my search history, changed my password to something wickedly obscure and set up a separate user ID and password for her. If there was one thing I could do better than her, it was computers. She was not getting anything else on me.

But I knew then that was it. Technically I could still vlog on the phone and iPad, edit secretly on the laptop when Leah wasn't doing her homework, but it would be harder and more rushed. And the thought of Leah following the channel and seeing everything I said online made things too awkward, too uncomfortable. I had to walk away from DBLG for good.

The following day was a Sunday – I took the camera equipment and three boxes of glitter over to Gloria's.

She opened the door and when she saw my face her eyes widened.

'Shit, Ellie, what happened to you?'

I burst into tears – big ugly sobs that left me unable to speak for five minutes. Gloria just put her arms around me, and right there in her hallway I just stood and bawled.

In the background I could hear the homey clatter of her mum making dinner, the babble of the telly, the sound of Keiran and his dad talking about football in the lounge. A proper, messy, normal, semi-happy blended family. My sobs got louder – the more I tried to control them the worse it got.

'Hun, what is it?'

I drew back, rummaged in my hoodie pocket for a tissue, tried to hold it together. And I lied. I made up a big row with David, Mum taking his side.

'I've taken the stepfamily diaries down from the channel,' I explained. I screwed the tissue tight into the corner of my eyes, seeing smudged mascara on there when I drew it back. 'I just can't risk them finding out and going apeshit. I want you to take over DBLG. I mean – I'll help with the behind-the-scenes stuff, but I can't go on camera any more.'

Gloria gave me a tight hug then she led me upstairs to her room – ushering me up there like a child who'd lost her way. She handed me some make-up remover wipes. I dabbed at my eyes until they were pink and sore, and then together we set about rebuilding my face from scratch.

Chapter 18

Leah

How can people bear it? The scrape, scrape of a nail file rasping against your fingers, the burned hair smell it produces. I'm usually good at smiling through uncomfortable things but this really puts me to the test. I've never been able to stand messing about with my fingernails.

Chelsea Rose, of Chelsea Rose Mobile Gel Art, leans forward and blows my fingertip, sending dust – tiny, white, filed-off bits of me – flying across our living room.

'How's that shape for you?' she asks.

Claire answers for me: I'm looking for something neat and simple apparently. Nothing too fancy or daring. Nothing that's going to be photographed close-up by the press and over-analysed as a reflection of my state of mind. No talons. Shame.

Curled up in the chair opposite, huge fluffy slippers on her feet, Ellie holds out her hand to photograph the sparkly-multicoloured-unicorn works of art she has chosen. Claire is policing her Amazing Children Awards look very closely – outfit colour, skirt length, hair dye – but with nails anything goes so Ellie has chosen the most outlandish look she can get away with.

Ellie catches me looking and glances away, as if she is afraid I'll take even this small pleasure away from her.

Not that I care what Ellie thinks of me. Of course I don't, I am just angry. What gives her the right to moan and complain? She is the one who came in and invaded my home, moving things around, poking about in my personal space. She lives in a precious, unbroken bubble where the biggest problem is that the fit arty boy with the murals doesn't really fancy her. She has time to think about nails and hair and clothes. She has a sweet and annoying little brother to fight with, a mother who indulges her. She has two parents – even if one of them moved to the other side of the world and started a new family.

Ugh. She's so demanding, so attention seeking, such a total unashamed diva.

I hate her. I really don't care one little bit what she thinks of me – I'm just ashamed I ever smiled at any of her jokes.

All my sympathy for her has long since burned into rage.

'Isn't this nice,' Claire says. 'All girls together.'

Thankfully neither Ellie nor I is required to answer – Claire and Chelsea fill the chasm. Nothing is nicer than a girly pampering session, Claire argues. Chelsea is wistful. She has three sons and wishes that she had a daughter to share her love of nail art with. Her youngest boy is starting to show an interest but she's not sure how she feels about that. Of course, she won't mind if he's gay (because obviously an interest in nails equals gay). Won't mind at all. But life would be so much easier for him if he wasn't, wouldn't it? So much prejudice.

'I understand,' Claire says, ever the people-pleaser, letting her off the homophobic hook. 'You just want a simple life for your kids.'

'*I* think it's cool,' Ellie virtue-signals from across the room.

I wonder for a moment what it would be like to speak my mind like Ellie, to pick apart Chelsea's argument with relentless logic and unleash just a tiny bit of rage on her. But after years of hiding my feelings and editing everything I say, my opinions are sealed up tight inside me, not for sharing. I keep quiet and hold out my hands for her to work on.

Chelsea Rose paints thick, even lines of pearly pink nail varnish on me. Seeing the layers of colour go on is strangely satisfying – my fingers look perfect, even and harmless, but the gel will dry hard and strong. I like it, although I wish I'd had the courage to choose the purple.

'That looks lovely,' Claire tells me unnecessarily. 'Doesn't it suit her skin tone, Ellie?'

Mention of skin tone puts us back on safe ground: The Great Spray-Tan Debate (Ellie: for; Claire: against) which rattles on for a good while until I hear Dad coming up the stairs, dropping his keys, muttering, ripping open his post as he comes. Then his head appears round the door. A frown line creases his forehead next to his left eye.

'What's all this?' His tone is playful but there's an uneasy edge. Claire is explaining about the treat, how fun it is to get ready for a party together.

'Of course,' he says. 'Pampering.'

He doesn't say anything else, but Claire gets it. Dad likes to think we're above that sort of thing. He wants us to look beautiful without even trying because trying means pretending. I wonder if he had these views when he was with Mum, or if these ideas, this fear of lies – even frivolous, well-meaning ones – seeped in afterwards.

Afterwards my fingers feel strangely heavy. I keep stroking them to feel the smooth, beetle-hard coating. Just for a short time, a few weeks, this tiny part of my body will be beautiful. The fumes have cleared, Chelsea has gone and Dad makes risotto while Claire grates cheese. Neither of them sees me standing by the doorway.

'It's our house, Claire,' he's saying. 'You never know who's going to take pictures and put them online.'

'I've known Chelsea since school,' Claire says. 'She'd never do anything like that. David, you've got to trust people.'

'It's not my job to trust people, it's my job to keep Leah safe.'

'David.' Claire's eyes are blazing now; her voice has gained strength but she's holding onto her temper. 'I'm not asking you to trust Chelsea, I'm asking you to trust *me* . . . Oh . . .'

They've seen me and freeze guiltily, shamefaced at the tiny flash of discord I have just seen. I know what will happen now and I am right. Dad puts his arm around Claire and gives her a squeeze. Claire smiles with her pink lips and they laugh nervously, trying to push away the note of wrongness in the air. A flash of memory comes back of a kitchen far away and long ago – Mum flinging an egg across the room at Dad's head, screaming names at him. Dad yelling back, his voice drowned out by me and Carey chanting the wonderful new words we'd just learned: 'POMPOUS-ARSE! POMPOUS-ARSE!' And then, as the yolk dripped down the fridge door they looked at each other and burst out laughing at the ridiculousness of it all.

Dad has forgotten how to do this, how to row one minute and make up the next. How long will it be before Claire figures out how broken we are?

I turn and go back to my hidey-hole. On a whim I spend some time on my phone's YouTube app checking out Dream Big Little Girl. Half the vlogs have vanished – it's just the puerile comedy and glitter-throwing ones now. The heart has been ripped out of it. I thumb through some of the other channels – Patricia Bright, Brogan Tate, that leopard-print woman. Faces in bedrooms across the world talking about their latest Primark purchase, what they've been up to this week. The kind of chat that you can hear on the top deck of a bus for nothing. I don't get it, I really don't. Why are these people interesting?

I keep flicking away, though. It's kind of hypnotic. They live in a different world – the way they're all friends with each other and gush on about each other's videos. My brain starts to wander off into a daydream where, instead of hiding my Amazing Children Awards dress in a black plastic sack in the storeroom, I bring it out, try it on and sashay about in front of my phone camera. *So, Leah fans, what do you think of my latest purchase?*

Would that have been me, if what happened hadn't happened?

Instead, my dress has remained a secret. I managed to brush off Claire's attempts to grill me on my outfit choice and Dad hasn't even thought to check that I'm not wearing the bridesmaid's dress again. He's really not a clothes person.

Much later I slip upstairs and dig the dress out, tiptoeing carefully down the hall so nobody sees. As I pass the sitting room, Dad, his voice gentle and contrite, is asking Claire to text the nail lady – just to make extra sure.

Next to me in the limo, Claire is fiddling with the complicated straps of her evening dress, checking her make-up, tweaking her lipstick. She thinks it's smudged, but that red mark on the bow of her lips is actually a spot. Every time she rubs it, it gets redder. I don't know what's worse – breaking the news that she has a spot, or letting her rub it until it blooms into a full-on carbuncle.

Dad is next to her, trying not to fidget in his suit. The shirt collar already looks grubby and his bow tie – a clip-on – is crooked. He is holding Claire's hand and glancing nervously at Dylan, who is playing with various gadgets on the limo control panel. I think Dad worries there may be an ejector seat. The newspaper sent this car, so it's not one of those pink palace hen-night things – it's for serious executives, as Dylan keeps telling us.

On the opposite side of the car sits my hapless victim Ellie, gazing out of the window at the passing traffic. Very little is remarkable about her this evening. She is wearing a nice black dress, moderate heels and carries a beaded clutch bag which has been searched and certified glitter-free. Claire thinks she is sulking because her gold strappy sandals were confiscated. Perhaps it is partly that – she really is that shallow – but mainly it's the blackmail.

I'm not nervous about getting her to make contact for me. I know she's foolish and clumsy and can't keep a secret to save her life, but she spent three months running an illicit vlog from her bedroom, the kind of vlog that could really damage our family, and guilt is a powerful motivator. What she also doesn't realise is that nobody will really be looking at her, especially once we're inside. It will be easy for her to slip away, out to where the photographers wait, restrained from setting foot on the red carpet by a couple of crash barriers. I'm sure he'll be there – he always is.

'Are you sure you don't want to take that fleece off yet?' Claire asks. I wrap it even closer around my shoulders and shake my head. I am trembling.

It's the dress. My beautiful black silken siren dress. A half hour before we were due to leave, I'd slipped it on in the mildewed confines of our bathroom. My shoulders and back felt chilly, goosebumps forming on skin I hadn't exposed since last year's trip to Cornwall. I felt raw, unprotected, a piece of meat for ogling. I realised I'd made a terrible mistake.

It was too late to change my mind and dig out Cousin Amber's rose-pink A-line number so I grabbed the brown fleece I wear around the house and wrapped it tight around me, so all anyone could see was the bottom part of the skirt. I scuttled into the car at the last minute so nobody could see.

'Let's see you,' Claire says now, beaming supportively.

I shake my head and she backs off. Dad glances at me as if for the first time and makes a comment about that being rather a lot of make-up.

'You know you have to, when there are photographers, otherwise your eyes look small and piggy in the pictures,' I say.

He looks saddened – but more by the modern world than by me.

We get out of the car and slip into the plush hotel venue through a side door – Amazing Children aren't subjected to the full red-carpet experience unless they choose to be. It helps protect us vulnerable types, and also ensures more exclusive shots for the newspaper sponsor – everyone's a winner. A man with a walkie-talkie headset hands us our passes and leads us to a long passageway, studded with chandeliers and expensive, perfumed floral arrangements. 'Cloakroom's that way.'

My heels wobble on the thick pile carpet and my legs feel weak. I feel trapped now, by my own stupid choice. How silly and shallow, to want to be pretty, to stand out from the crowd for a different reason. To be *grown up*. I blame Ellie. When I picked out the dress, she was the one in my mind. I knew she'd like it – which should have been enough of a signal to stop me buying it.

We're in the cloakroom now, a large room with a snaking queue of courageous children and their parents. Dads overwhelmed by the décor and the friendly cloakroom staff, mums in brand-new frocks with matchy-matchy clutch bags and shoes, younger kids not remotely bothered by their surroundings and climbing all over the gilt furniture.

There are all sorts of dresses here – puffy ones, voluminous ones, floor-length, knee-length. Women with fascinators, men struggling with cummerbunds and bow ties, muttering about how much they hate this formal stuff.

Hoping to stay inconspicuous, I slither out of the fleece. Claire takes it without really looking – and then she does a double take.

'Wow, Leah—'

'Please don't say wow.' I hunch my shoulders and try to make myself small. I wish I wasn't so gangly.

'No, darling, you look lovely.'

What I look, as I realised in that bathroom back home, is sexy. Not slutty or sleazy or anything – just slick, more adult than I've ever looked before. I never set out to do it, but that's what happened. The naked flesh on my shoulders and back prickles, as if I can feel people's eyes on it already.

Dad, who was chatting to one of the security guards, turns round and I see his mouth fall open, his eyes a strange mixture of pride, disappointment and confusion.

'Leah . . .' He doesn't know what to say. 'I don't know if you should be wearing that,' he finishes lamely.

I realise everyone in the cloakroom area is looking at me. My face burns but the rest of me is cold – I draw my arms across my chest. Fight-or-flight panic kicks in and I start to gather up my clutch bag, my fleece. I can see that Dad would take me home without a single question asked. In fact, it would make him relieved – he would probably rather hide away with his books than be seen in public with his daughter's shoulders.

I glance at Ellie – she has cracked a smile for the first time this evening. A reluctant lopsided curve of the lip. I meet her eye and for a moment there is a connection. She gets it – and yes, she likes the dress.

The contact lasts less than a moment before we both remember the blackmail. I can't go home and give Ellie a chance to squirm out of her duty this evening. Somehow, I will have to get through the night.

Just then I think about my little sister. I remember her draped in Mum's floral dressing gown with a plastic tiara and a sparkly sequinned handbag in the crook of her arm. A tiny Cinderella who never got to go to the ball. As I think of that, my back straightens, my lips press together in a slight smile.

'Let's go in.'

Chapter 19

Ellie

I heard it first – the low hum of people chit-chatting, the chink of champagne glasses. I even thought I heard the whispering sound of silk and satin gowns on bare, cellulite-free celebrity legs. The doors to the main hall opened and there it was, a room I'd only seen on television before. I recognised the heavy crystal chandeliers on the ceiling but now I was really here, standing in the balcony bar looking down on a room full of white cotton discs – dining tables set with polished silver and covered with flowers. Scanning the bar, at first all I could see was beautiful dresses – glittering splashes of colour, glimpses of boob and thigh from the reality stars. I remembered reading somewhere that celebrities have to wear colour on the red carpet as it helps them stand out – silently I kicked myself for letting Mum talk me into my short, black dress.

A familiar-looking woman in a pink gown walked past and I raised my hand to wave at her, only to realise to my mortification that I'd just 'hiya'd' the winner of last year's *Strictly*. After that the faces above the dresses snapped into focus. There was the *Made in Chelsea* cast. There was the woman from *Line of Duty* and ... oh my God – VLOGGERS. Xav Bailey and Ed, Leni Loves ... All the biggies were here, standing together in a group of beautiful, successful gorgeousness. My legs were trembling, fighting the urge to run up to them, drool all over them and pump them for advice.

I had forgotten everything – the blackmail, the bizarre shock of Sexy Leah and the whole last three months in the stinking shop. Every bone in my body was screaming: THIS IS WHERE I BELONG.

I will be famous. I will get here under my own steam. I will.

Mum nudged my arm. 'Isn't that that girl you like?' She pointed over to where a broad, sweeping staircase led down from the bar towards the dining tables. There, in an incredibly foxy silver slip dress and leopard heels was MaxineF – and she was waving at me.

I jumped about a foot in the air – fuelled by a weird cocktail of pride, excitement and sheer panic.

'Does she know you?' Mum asked.

'Course not.' The lie shot out of my mouth. 'I think she's waving at that woman from *Hollyoaks*.'

David came over holding some champagne flutes with orange juice in and together we raised a toast to our new family. Leah clinked my glass and leaned in towards me. Her hair smelled sweet and expensive – up close I could see the soft, fine hairs under her cheekbones, dusted with a coating of face powder.

'The paps might leave soon,' she murmured. 'You need to go now. Do you remember the description I gave you?'

I nodded, the sick feeling coming back.

I made some crack about going off to stalk the YouTubers. Mum smiled – probably relieved to see me relax. I started off across the room towards them, then ducked out and hared off towards the hotel foyer.

The sheer grandness of it stopped me short for a minute – chandeliers, gold everywhere, marble clicky-clacky floor. I wanted to rush around stroking the leather chairs and making unnecessary phone calls from the antique wooden telephone booths in the corner, but there wasn't time. I headed for the huge archway of a front door.

Leah had explained that the whole event was sponsored by one newspaper and their official photographers were covering the event from inside. In order to get tickets for all of us, David had agreed to an exclusive family group shot for the newspaper. Meanwhile all the photographers from other media would be camped out at the front door, desperate to get a glimpse of some inappropriate celebrity cleavage as they made their way into the awards. This guy she wanted me to meet would be on the outside.

The entrance was heavily guarded – security, events people with clipboards, hotel staff in white shirts and dicky-bows. Luckily, they were there to stop people coming in rather than going out. Channelling the Hollywood A-list, I strode past them like I knew where I was going and out onto the red carpeted steps, towards a black, buzzing hive of camera lenses – which all lifted as one and pointed right at me.

I tingled. So this was how it felt.

Unfortunately it only lasted a couple of seconds – the cameras lowered back down and the paparazzi didn't bother to hide their disappointment.

Now the cameras were lowered, I could see there weren't actually that many of them but they were still a pretty intimidating bunch. They kind of looked like off-duty soldiers with cameras instead of machine guns and most of them were men, although there was an amazing-looking woman with wild hair and ripped jeans who I basically wanted to *be*. And there was a man talking to her.

I half hoped it wasn't really him. Then I could run back to Leah and honestly say that I tried. But then what would happen? More blackmail? It did look like him, though – I grabbed my phone out of my clutch bag and checked the Google image Leah had given me. Yep. He was older, greyer and holding an e-cig, but that was him.

I stumbled down the steps and slipped past the barrier, squirming between bodies until I was standing next to him.

Now – how *does* one pass on a secret message from your blackmailing stepsister to a news-hungry photographer? I tugged his sleeve meekly.

'Erm . . . I think I need to talk to you about a story.'

It only took a couple of moments to drag him off to one side where I could pass on Leah's message. He seemed completely bemused by it, kept asking 'Are you *sure*?' I felt sorry for the guy – I had no idea what she was up to either, so all I could do was shrug and insist that that's what she'd said. I even had to show him a photo of me with Leah on my phone to prove I was who I said I was. By the end he was convinced and looked depressingly honoured by Leah's deigning to notice him.

Mission accomplished. Now to get back inside before anyone noticed I was missing. By now most of the press pack had disappeared – the long shadows of the remaining photographers stretched out across the red carpet. I ran back up the steps – right into the line of official clipboardy types.

'I'm afraid the hotel lobby is closed for an event,' a woman said.

They had to be kidding.

'But I just came out! You must have seen me?'

The clipboards looked blankly at me. How could they have missed me? Was my outfit really so ordinary? Was I that forgettable? Then one – a slightly younger one with a blonde, straggly ponytail and a sympathetic face – stepped forward. 'Do you have your invitation?'

Of course I didn't. And my name wasn't on the list, either – I was one of David and Leah Stoke's plus-three.

Giving up, I whirled around on my heels, ran back down the steps and round to the side entrance we'd come in before. Surely the security guard there would remember me?

The side road was dark and jammed up with posh-looking taxis waiting for the event to end. The side door – which had been flung open in a pool of light before – was now firmly shut.

By now my stupid formal black shoes were pinching – yet again I cursed Mum for not letting me wear my super comfy gold gladiators. I slipped out of them and laid my bare feet on the horrible greasy step to cool down while I got out my phone and dialled Leah.

No answer. Of course not – that thing she was wearing definitely did not have pockets.

Shit.

Deep breaths. Unlocking my phone again I accepted my fate and called Mum.

Naturally, it caused a huge stink. It wasn't Mum who came up to the foyer to vouch for me, it was David – his name was the one on the list, after all. His lips were pressed together in a tight, straight line and he kept running his fingers through his lank hair as he explained things to the blonde clipboard girl. His bow tie was even more crooked than before.

'We were looking for you,' he said. 'The newspaper wanted us for pictures half an hour ago and now the ceremony has started it might be too late. Really, Ellie, I wasn't sure you were ready for this kind of responsibility, but I'm disappointed that I was proved right.'

Of all the prissy, up-himself, dickish things to say ... I walked faster, on through the corridors to the function room, my feet raw and tears bubbling up behind my eyes as David trotted to keep up with me. As we reached the main event room again, I couldn't hold it in any more, and whirled around to face him. 'You're not my dad,' I snapped. 'Dad would never talk to me like that. Never.'

I thought saying something would stop me from blubbing but it actually made things much worse – speaking the truth unleashed a hideous wave of sobs, of hot, bitter, mascara-destroying tears. In the background I could hear someone speaking over the PA system, a rising swell of inspirational music. But I could feel people's eyes turning away from the screen and towards me. My face blazing with shame, I ran.

Even as I fled I was trying not to cause too much fuss – skirting round the edge of those big white dining tables, away from the celebrities and the brave children with bigger problems than mine. I eventually saw a gilt mahogany sign for *Ladies' Cloakroom* and slammed my way inside, past the shiny mirrors and marble sinks and into a cubicle, where I really let rip with the sobs.

I just couldn't stop. In my head a list of everything wrong with my life repeated over and over – the pressure-cooker atmosphere of the shop; the fallout with my friends; Leah's blackmail; letting go of the vlogs. I screwed up some toilet paper and jammed it into the corner of my eyes, making them sore as I soaked up the make-up and tears.

Somehow I had to get out of here, walk alone through a roomful of strangers and possibly go on to pose for a photograph that would appear in a national newspaper. I couldn't face it. Maybe I could just live in this toilet cubicle – it seemed nice enough.

Then there was a gentle tap at the door.

'Ellie, are you in there?' Mum's voice. I didn't think I could face her but slowly I slid the bolt on the door, eyes lowered with shame. There were Mum's shoes and next to them a pair of leopard-print ones.

My shame deepened even further. 'M-Maxine?'

'I hope you don't mind,' Maxine said. 'I saw you dash in here and you looked upset so I went to get your mum.'

I shut the cubicle door again, sank back onto the toilet lid. But Maxine and Mum coaxed me out between them and then sat me on an elaborate silk-covered sofa in the corner. Mum dabbed some cold water on my eyes with a napkin while Maxine told a string of salacious stories about vloggers to distract me until finally I calmed down enough to talk. She didn't mention the collab or even the big glaring thing that I had neglected to tell her while we were working together – the small detail of who my stepsister actually was. But I knew Mum wasn't stupid and she must be wondering how we knew each other. I was going to have a lot of explaining to do.

After about ten minutes Maxine gave a gasp and looked at her tiny silver watch, saying she was due in the Green Room and that she'd message me. I thanked her again and then she was gone, leaving Mum and me looking at each other, one big fat secret between us.

'Mum, I . . .'

'Oh, Ellie, I know. I've known for weeks. It's your fault – you got me thinking that I needed to get some of these YouTubies involved in CAREY so I googled around until I found your channel thing. Dream Big Little Girl – the song your father wrote for you.' Her voice sounded tired, but she wasn't yelling, which made me feel better.

I told her I'd taken it all down.

Well, most of it.

Well, some of it.

'What are you going to do?' I asked. 'Are you going to tell Dave?'

Mum slumped forward, her head in her hands. 'I don't know. I really don't know.'

I'd never heard Mum say anything like that before. She always knew what to do. Even when Dad left. Even when my teachers complained about my behaviour when I started secondary school. Even when we moved in with David and Leah. She smoothed things over and made things right. It's what she always did. But David would be devastated if he found out she'd been keeping my secret for weeks. I suddenly got a flash of what it was like to be her, tiptoeing around her traumatised partner, trying to understand everything he'd been through while also trying to coax him out into the real world.

I could have told her everything then, handed over the whole big Leah mess to her and feel the weight of all those secrets lift. The teddy bear, the Bible, the blackmail – everything. But she looked so tired, so helpless, that I realised that this time she didn't have the answers. I wasn't even sure David would believe me, especially once he knew about the vlog. No, I knew at that moment that there was only one thing I could do. I had to pose for a photograph and smile my face off for the cameras.

In the end, I don't know why we bothered. The family photo was a tiny insert on page twelve – my face was smaller than my Twitter profile photo on my phone and I didn't even get any extra followers. The whole right-hand side of page one was dedicated to a photograph of Leah, back to camera and smiling that dazzling smile over one perfect shoulder. THE FACE OF COURAGE GROWS UP.

Chapter 20

Leah

For someone who loves being at the centre of a drama, Ellie does not look happy as she slides into the booth next to me. She has chosen to arrange the meeting in a bog-standard Italian café near the train station so the photographer wouldn't have to travel far. The interior is all mirrored walls, ripped red pleather booths and chipped curved metal bistro chairs, old copies of *The Sun* tucked behind neglected pot plants and a flirty guy at the counter. It's called Puccini's or Panini's or something else with an apostrophe. I order the spag bol, Ellie has an apple.

'I picked here because it has booths,' Ellie says. 'Thought it would be more private. What do you reckon?'

I don't bother answering as I don't have anything to say.

'Right.' 'Well done, Ellie, smart thinking.'' Ellie's voice goes all breathy; she pouts and tosses her hair. To be honest, it's not a bad impression of me.

I can't help it – I laugh just a bit. Ellie sees the tiny crack I've let show and takes it as a cue to talk more.

'You really should stop sneering at everything,' she says. 'Life's more fun if you keep an open mind. Treat everything like an adventure.'

Ugh. I hate that kind of Insta-Wisdom, but her words still carry a sting. I get that unnerving feeling again, the thought that sometimes Ellie isn't completely stupid. I push the idea away. I cannot let myself get distracted for more than a split second – there will be no second chances, and I don't want to mess this up. The photographer is called Pete Stone. He's well respected in newspaper circles and his Twitter account has a healthy following of hardcore snappers and media studies students. According to his profile, he has a wife and three kids.

I realise suddenly that Ellie has fallen silent and her face has tensed into a serious expression that looks like a pout on her.

'Are you sure you know what you're doing?' she asks me.

I give her a Shut-Up-Ellie look. Nobody asked her to be here, in fact I've told her more times than I can count that her attendance is not required. I only needed her to set up the meeting, not be at it, but she refused to tell me the time or the place unless I brought her along. Considering she has done her best to avoid me for months, I don't know what the hell she thinks she's doing.

'Just play along with me,' I tell her. 'Why couldn't you just stay at home?'

Her lips press together as if she is fighting with all her might to stop talking, holding back a tsunami of prattle about soap stars and school and feelings. I still can't believe she's so close to me in age.

Could she do what I was planning to do? Not in a million years.

I push the thought away. When I was a child I plotted constantly, writing everything down, drawing pictures of my worst nightmares. Later there were diaries, letters and the thoughts I sent out to Crow as we both drifted off to sleep at night.

But as the time for action got closer, it became less necessary to repeat every fine detail, over and over again. Now, I find it much easier not to think of it, to create a wall in my mind around it – no route in, no route out. The feel and shape of what I have done and what I want to do can stay there, waiting like a particularly nasty Christmas present – until I need to unwrap it. It's the only way to stop myself from turning back. Besides, there is no point examining it from every angle – the decision has been made years ago, my course was set in stone the moment Crow did what he did.

No, it went back further than that. To the park, the library, the stationery shop, Kentucky . . .

Stop. Breathe.

The café door opens with a cheery jingle. Over the brass top of the booth I see the crown of his head – a forest of spiked, salt-and-pepper hair. He walks over to the counter without looking over at us and orders himself a black coffee. He's wearing a black bomber jacket which looks expensive even though it's out of fashion. He isn't carrying his usual camera bag with all his prying long-lens gadgetry but instead has a small one slung over his shoulder like a black, shiny comfort blanket. Perhaps he feels naked without one – he probably thinks I won't notice it there.

I become aware that my breathing has quickened, my hands are shaking slightly. I quickly clasp them together in front of me. *Stop it – I have to be stronger than this.*

I turn to Ellie. 'Distract him for a few seconds when he first sits down,' I say. 'I need time.'

Ellie rolls her eyes muttering to herself: 'First she says shut up, then she says talk . . .'

Then the photographer is here, lowering his paunchy self into the padded bench opposite me, arranging his coffee just so. He smiles – a different one to his photoshoot smile, more nervous somehow.

Without pausing to let him stir his coffee, Ellie starts to bombard him with questions about celebrities. Who is lovely? Who is a diva? Who has cellulite and who's had work done? Did he know if there was any truth in the rumours about Blah Blah and her secret eating disorder? She crunches her apple and beams at him – her teeth are brilliant white and for a moment she really does look like a star, just playing the part of an overly naïve teenager.

I eat my pasta slowly and deliberately, not thinking about The Thing. Instead I focus on all the times I've seen Pete Stone before. At a photo shoot in a field, at the Amazing Children Awards and the Marathon. There has always been a protective layer between us – a few feet of pavement, a crash barrier, Dad fluttering around. I've never been this close to him. His shirt is unbuttoned at the top and a tangle of white chest hairs bristles out at the neck. Nestled by his left sideburn there's a large brown mole which must be a pain to shave around. There is a thick, battered gold wedding ring on his left hand with a Celtic pattern and he smells of too much aftershave; it tickles my nose and makes me want to sneeze.

There, he is human, just like everyone else – except me and Crow.

I can see he's starting to get uncomfortable – he hasn't come here to trade D-list gossip with a wannabe. Pete's grey eyes meet mine over Ellie's head and I suddenly know that I need to talk first, otherwise he will – and then he'll be in charge of the conversation.

'Thanks for coming,' I say.

I've thought about this conversation very carefully, but I still feel unsure of the best way to work it. Still, I've got to start somewhere, so I decide to make my offer first and let him figure out that there is a price. I lay it out. In a month's time, I am turning eighteen. Grown up at last, coming of age, key of the door, yada yada. Time for me to take control and tell my own story.

I offer him everything. A photo shoot, a makeover (Tragic Leah Stoke as you've never seen her before!), a full interview. I even drop hints about a boyfriend – Ellie squirms in her seat when she hears that one, but she keeps her trap clamped shut as if I have a vice on it. I've never felt this kind of power before – the power of someone being afraid of me. I have to say, I quite like it.

Pete Stone's eyes widen, the muscles in his jaw tighten – he is overwhelmed, and it's not surprising. The photos at the award ceremony made the whole world realise that I wasn't a child any more and this makes me a story again. Since then, the CAREY offices have been inundated with well-wishers and, inexplicably, more teddy bears, but most of all with requests for an interview, a photo shoot. So I know the value of what I'm offering.

For a couple of moments the photographer struggles to speak.

'Are you sure this is what you want?'

The compassion in his voice surprises me. It doesn't sound fake or persuasive. He is genuinely giving me a get-out clause.

I nod. 'I feel like I know you,' I tell him, letting my eyes widen to show sincerity. 'You've always been there, you always seemed nice and friendly, so I think you'll take care of me. And I need my voice to be heard.'

I realise as I speak that I really do think I know him, just as he probably thinks he knows me, and that we are probably both wrong.

Should I really sucker him into this?

Needs must.

I cast my eyes down, twisting a sugar cube between my fingers as I speak. 'Especially now. Now he's out.'

I feel Ellie tense up next to me but she still doesn't say anything. I keep talking, drawing Pete Stone closer to what I want, saying that I don't feel safe, I can't believe he's out so soon and how can I be so sure he's been rehabilitated?

He is sympathetic – he makes a little gesture like he wants to reach out and take my hand, and for a moment I think

178

about letting him, just to get him to say what I want. But at the last moment I draw back, folding my hands on my lap. He mirrors my gesture – that's what people like him do to get people like me to relax.

I keep on talking. 'After all, it's an open secret where he lives,' I say. All the press know about this seaside town where he has made his new home. It seems unjust that nobody will tell me.

'It would help to know where,' I say, with just the right level of pathetic tremor in my voice. 'Especially if it was far away.'

He draws breath, moistens his lip with his tongue, hesitates. Those few heartbeats last an age. I feel hot and flushed, I struggle to hold my emotions in. I want to fly over the table, grab his bomber jacket collar and scream into his face: 'TELL ME!'

He tells me.

I kid you not, it really was that easy. He even tells me Crow's new name – Sam Clarke – and the name of the estate he lives on. It's not precise but it's enough to get me started.

'I think you have a right to know,' he says. 'You're right, you're an adult and I think it's outrageous he's been allowed to hide away. And besides . . .' He hesitates for a moment and then decides to keep going. 'My youngest daughter would have been the same age as you this year. Drunk driver. The bloke got fourteen years, out in seven.'

I tell him I'm sorry, knowing exactly how pointless those words are.

We move onto safer ground, the type of shoot I would want. In central London, with none of those childish props around me. No hair ribbons, no teddy bears or ponies.

'Not that I want raunchy either,' I say, throwing in a shy, crooked smile. 'But then you know me well enough not to do that.'

He is all reassurance.

It is becoming harder to concentrate because Ellie has put her hand on my leg and is gripping it, hard. I glance down and can see her knuckles are white and she is digging her finger-nails into my jeans. I can't feel them through the denim, but the contact itself is unnerving. I can count on the fingers of one hand the number of people who have touched me physically in the last ten years. It's even on the list of Rules. Nobody but Ellie – and possibly her mother – would have the gall to do it.

Next to me she still has a smile on her face, and her eyes are still sparkling and locked on the photographer, but there's a giveaway, a twitch in the muscles around her mouth that shows she is now worried. The Diva is not stupid.

I keep up my performance, give the photographer a Gmail address I have no intention of checking and thank him for being there for me. He thanks me for the opportunity and reassures me once again that he is different, he can be trusted – I have come to the right person.

Ellie is subdued but she does manage to ask him one more pointless celebrity question before he leaves.

The two of us catch the bus back together – there is no avoiding it as I am too exhausted to think of ways to shake her off. I lean my head against the grubby window, my hair makes whirling patterns in the condensation as I look out at the passing rainy mediocrity – the yellow streetlights, blurs of people going about their business. Ellie fidgets with a game on her phone.

She tries to form the sentence three or four times, without looking up from the screen. Her fingers flick pixelated balloons into colour-coded groups of red, green and purple as she speaks. She must find it easier to talk to me without looking me in the eye. 'You're not . . .' she says, 'I mean, you . . .' and finally it blurts out in one clumsy line. 'Don't do anything stupid, Leah.'

I turn to face her and raise an eyebrow, daring her to say anything more. She keeps her eyes fixed on the game and I go back to the grimy view.

As soon as I turn away, she takes a breath to talk again. Of course.

'Since when was it your business, Ellie?' I ask before she can speak. 'Just go back to your vlogging or whatever and leave me alone.'

Flick, flick. Blue balloons burst in a shower of stars and unicorns and extra bonus points. Somewhere in Ellie's brain a reward centre lights up, which is probably why she doesn't just let it go.

'Look, I don't care what you do,' she says. 'But I've seen the stuff that goes on in your head. I found your teddy bear with those drawings inside it, and OK, I nosed around, but I'm glad I did now. You can't just . . .'

I'm sitting bolt upright now, staring at her. 'Where's Kentucky?'

She looks blank, stutters something about the American south and for a moment the blood is pumping too much in my ears to realise the crossed wires. I grab her shoulder. Why not? She grabbed me first.

'The bear. Where is he – it?'

I feel sick, exposed, like she's reached into my guts and is just rummaging around in there looking for extra bonus points.

'Leah, this is mental. You can't really be planning to do all that stuff?'

I feel the sudden urge to grab her by the throat. Grab her and shake, shake shake. But the person I'm really angry at is me. *I thought I'd sealed him in, I thought nobody would ever find that panel under the wardrobe.*

I'd shoved him somewhere dark, dusty and tight and hoped never to see him again, then I locked the memory of him away, along with everything else, in the part of my brain with the Do Not Touch sign on it. I should have let Dad burn him. No, I should have burned him myself – another test of my toughness.

I sink my head into my hands, my brain can't cope with this, not straight after the photographer. I push the balls of my palms into my eye sockets, hard, until I can see lights pulse on the inside of my eyelids. I do it to play for time, to think of a way to talk my way out of this and to stop myself from smashing Ellie's wide-open face into one of the bus poles.

I feel a gentle, hesitant pressure on my shoulder – Ellie is stroking it carefully, ready to pull her hand away at any moment – the way you might try to comfort a dangerous dog. She thinks I am crying and I realise that that is how I have to play it. I bite down on my lip and sniff loudly.

'Leah don't, I didn't mean it.'

I try to shake off her hand, brushing my hair over my eyes so she can't see that they are dry.

'I'm fine,' I tell her, sniffing again. 'That bear was the one I had with me when . . .'

A tiny *oh* escapes her like a sigh. Her hand slithers down and back onto her lap. She is dumb with shock and for a moment so am I. I did not intend to offer her a piece of the truth, but it came out and now it has escaped, a part of me feels lighter. Giving another fragment couldn't hurt, could it?

'Those pictures helped me a long time ago,' I said. 'They're in the past. But I couldn't quite bring myself to destroy them, or the bear. I mean it, I'd like it back, please.'

Ellie breathes out, long and slow, sits back in her seat. I can feel some of the tension leaving her.

'Of course,' she says. 'I'm sorry – I found it in my room. I didn't mean to pry – well, not at first.' She laughs, an irritating little trill. 'I really thought you were planning to do something but I should have known better. You're not that stupid.'

The moment we climb the stairs to the flat, I can feel a difference in the atmosphere. Ellie senses it too – a stillness, a quietness. Dad and Claire meet us out in the hallway, a tense greeting party. Claire's eyes look red, the corners of her mouth pulled tight.

'Oh, there you are, love,' Dad says, his tone wooden. Claire fusses around us, offering cups of tea and chocolate biscuits.

'Claire,' Dad says, and she freezes for a moment, before rushing to the kitchen, her face turned away from us. Dad asks me to go downstairs for a while, saying he wants to talk to Ellie *privately*. That's when I notice he hasn't looked at her – not once since we came in.

Ah. So that's it. Poor Ellie – all that blackmail and they found out anyway.

To my surprise, Ellie moves closer to me, her shoulder touching mine, ever so slightly in my shadow. That little movement lights a tiny flare of protectiveness in me – I am allowed to mess with her, but heaven help anyone else who does. I call through to the kitchen, telling Claire I'd like that cup of tea after all.

Minute after agonising minute passes. I guess in normal families they'd be having a screaming knock-down row right now. Instead Dad is squirming, tying himself in knots trying to act natural until I am out of the way. I decide not to play his game.

'Dad, if this is about Ellie's YouTube thing . . .'

And then everyone is speaking at once, jangling argument against argument. Ellie screeching excuses and justifications and talking about her human rights, Dad bellowing in self-righteous judgement, Claire begging everyone to calm down, thrusting a tea mug into my hand and rushing between the two of them as if to push them apart.

'Please David, you're overreacting—'

'I can't talk to you right now, Claire. You knew – you *knew* what she was up to and you didn't do anything.'

My heart is thumping and my body floods with a weak, watery feeling. I want to scream, to sob, to beg everyone to stop talking before they ruin everything.

But it's out of control now. I haven't seen Dad shout for years and it's as if someone has flipped the top off a badly shaken Coke bottle – he can't stop, he can't hold anything in. He's shouting about the crowded flat, Dylan's pointless computer games, Claire's air freshener habit and now he's calling Ellie names – vapid, air-headed, fame whore.

At that last word Ellie reels back as if she's been punched in the face. But it's Claire who speaks – teeth bared, holding tight onto Ellie's shoulders.

'Get out, David. Get out now.'

Dad's face crumbles, too angry and full of his own hurt to understand what he's done wrong. He whirls away, downstairs to the shop. I follow him – not to talk to him but to climb the ladder to the Hole. He lets me go, doesn't even try to explain. A few moments later the bell tinkles and I hear the shop door close behind him.

So this is how it ends. A failed experiment in normal life for the Stoke family. I lie there with a book in my hands, the print swimming in front of me. I am tired. Tired of being protected and cushioned and cosseted. Tired of the teddy bears, the photo shoots in cornfields and, most of all, the pretending.

I am not what they think I am. I am not a victim, I am not weak. I'm not a nice, good girl who is only happy when curled up with a good book. I don't want their protection or their weepy sympathy. I want to hurt something.

There is nothing here for me any more – not even the ghost of a family. I might as well just do it now.

I unwrap that nasty Christmas present in my head.

Chapter 21

Ellie

For a couple of blissful moments after I opened my eyes, the world felt normal. A shaft of dim sunlight poked its way through the curtains and sliced across the heart-shaped crack in the ceiling. The Baptist church across the street had already flung open its doors and groups of keen early worshippers were walking noisily by under my window. My mind spooled off into plans for the day – *Sunday afternoon shopping with Gloria maybe, unless Mum wants to do that family roast dinner thing again . . .*

Oh. Oh shit.

Reality seeped back in and I went cold.

My phone said it was 8 a.m. but there was no sign of movement yet. No clatter of breakfast from the kitchen or the groaning pipes which meant that someone was having a shower. Yesterday's clothes were pooled by my bed and I dragged them straight on, pulling on my grey jeans and trying to ignore the whiff on my cold-shoulder shirt.

Crouching on the floor I pulled out the small glittery suitcase I'd last used on a school trip to France. I packed it without really thinking about why, or even where I was going. I was just going away. Maybe Billie or Gloria's at first for a few days. After that I didn't know – did they let under-eighties into Gran's sheltered accommodation? Or maybe it was time to cash in my savings and fly out to see Dad . . . but then what about exams next year? Maybe – hope fluttered inside my belly at this – he'd come back to England for a few months and help me sort things out.

This would need proper thinking time, and I couldn't do that here.

There was no way I could stay at the shop, not after what David said. Not just because he was being a dick of epic proportions but because of the sick, heavy feeling of pressure that I'd felt there for the past few months. It was there because of me. Even before I fucked up, it felt like the whole family was waiting for me to do something wrong without even knowing it.

After David left, Mum told me it wasn't her who had dobbed me in – it was one of the CAREY volunteers whose darling daughter Hermione had shown her the MaxineF vlog. She'd recognised me and phoned David – all out of concern for Leah's welfare, of course, and nothing to do with jealousy of Mum, or a gleeful delight in causing trouble. No, she was far too high-minded for that.

Mum had done a lot of crying and made a lot of excuses for David. He'd been protecting Leah for years, he'd got carried away, didn't know what he was saying. 'He actually really likes you,' she'd said. 'You make him laugh.'

'If you ask me, he's about the worst possible person to run a charity that's all about raising awareness and getting publicity,' I'd said. 'He should be lining up to go on YouTube, not hiding away from it.'

Mum went quiet at that, and whether I was right or wrong it was clear I just didn't fit in with this new two-in-one family. It would be easier for them with me gone – Mum and David would patch things up, Dylan and Leah could become closer friends. And as for me, I wouldn't have to be ashamed of my real self any more.

The suitcase was full in almost no time – I threw my iPad, laptop and chargers on top and squeezed it shut, forcing the zip closed. With any luck I'd get out of here without having to confront anyone. This was one dramatic scene I would rather avoid.

As I swung my case onto the floor, I noticed the grey-brown furball crammed into the corner of my sock drawer. What had she called that bear? Kentucky. What a weird name. I wished I'd never found it. I wish I'd just left Leah alone, like she'd wanted all along.

Too late for that now.

I'd give the bear back before I left. Hopefully I'd be able to leave it outside her hidey-hole without disturbing her. I tucked it under one arm and lifted the suitcase – the wheels would make too much noise on the hallway rugs. The flat smelled of last night's takeaway, the kitchen strewn with Canton Moon food boxes, sticky sweet pools of leftovers still inside and bits of noodle stuck to the table and the floor. Dylan and I had eaten in silence with Mum, then disappeared to our rooms after.

I thought about Mum getting up to this – David and me both gone and mess everywhere. But it couldn't be helped. If I stayed to clear it up, somebody might wake up and stop me. I grabbed a Diet Coke out of the fridge and tiptoed down the stairs.

The shop was its normal, grotty self. Morning sun streamed in through the front windows, a cardboard box of books lay by David's counter ready for sorting. I left the suitcase next to it and climbed the steps to Leah's hideout as quietly as I could, so as not to wake her.

I pulled the ragged little curtain open a crack and propped the bear just inside with a sense of relief.

The relief lasted about two seconds. Because then I saw Leah's things were gone. No postcards, no suitcase, no discarded clothes. Not even a note.

A feeling of horror crept over me as I realised where she was going, what she might be about to do. The thought of it blew everything else out of the water – the vlog, the fight with David, the wedding.

My body was moving before I'd even had time to think about it. I scrambled down the splintery wooden steps, fumbling for my door keys, fingers like rubber.

As I struggled, I heard the shop door open. I looked up, hoping to see Leah's long curtain of hair and miserable face. Instead, David was standing there. He looked like shit.

'Ellie, I'm so sorry, please let me explain . . .'

Then he clocked the suitcase next to me and his expression changed to one of horror.

*　　*　　*

The options were spinning out in front of me. I could stay, I could tell David what happened, waste a day having endless serious conversations, analysing Where We Went Wrong, taking the blame for keeping quiet about it all and watching helplessly as he called the police in to bring her back. Or I could just go.

I launched out, barging clumsily past him, bashing both our legs with the case as I crammed myself through the front door.

'Ellie, please . . .' he called.

No time. I shouted back over my shoulder as I ran along the pavement. 'Leah's gone – but it's OK, David, I know where she's going. I'll get her! I'll stop her!'

Chapter 22

Boyd, before

I'm not following her. No really, this time I'm not. I am stalking Tony.

I asked around the Crew, found out Tony had got himself a job working for a mate, washing cars in a shopping centre car park.

An actual job. That won't bloody last, I thought to myself. Then Bart pointed out that car parks are dark, that there are places to hide and spaces between the cars where CCTV doesn't reach.

I had to do something – the others would never let up if I didn't.

I stand there all fucking morning hidden down the side of a grey Transit van, watching Tony scrubbing and Squeegee-ing, flicking water at his mates and laughing, stretched out on the buff leather front seat of a Merc, pretending he owns it.

I'm shaking – whether it's rage or fear or what I don't know, but I wish I could kill him with my eyes, the arrogant bastard. The knife is in my pocket, the handle hot and clammy from where I've been gripping it so hard.

'Come on asswipe, it'll take two seconds,' Troy sneers. 'Run in, stab, run out.'

'Stab twice,' Bart adds. 'For good measure.'

'You don't need it,' Frankie says. 'Just angle the knife upwards under the ribs.' Someone in the Crew had told us once that's how you do it – I don't know if they were bullshitting or telling the truth. I've never stabbed anyone. Been in lots of fights, had a knife pulled on me, but I don't know how a blade feels when it goes into a body. Is it like cutting into butter or slicing a steak? *There's only one way to find out*, they all say.

I chew on my lip until it hurts, squeeze my eyes shut trying to block them out. When I open them, he's standing right there in front of me.

'Fuck me, it's Boyd.' He's smiling like he's missed me, front tooth even more crooked than it was before. There's an e-fag clutched in his meaty fist, which explains why he smells of strawberries. The others go mad, like, screaming at me to *do it, do it do it*.

'It's Crow now,' is all I manage to say. I'm fighting to keep still as he considers my new name then shakes his head, throwing all I've become aside with a laugh. He holds out his arms as if he's going to hug me. I pull back instinctively and he laughs again and asks after my mum. There's a note in his voice that makes it sound like he owns her, that he has some kind of right to know and that he's forgotten how she was the last time he saw her – utterly broken down by grief.

Now is the time. Peak anger. Peak hate. Hidden by the van. Knife in my hand.

Do it, do it, do it.

Tony senses something's off, his body shifts slightly from friendly to attack mode. His shoulders seem broader, his smile lazy and wicked, and suddenly it's there rushing up through my body – the sheer terror of him. My breath comes in short gasps, I can't speak.

I run.

Through the car park, up the stairs. I don't stop until the soft jangly music of the mall hits me. I lean back against the fire doors and double over, retching until I throw up on the shiny floor. Shoppers pass me by, making little noises of disgust and I move on, wiping my mouth on my sleeve, not caring. The screeching fury of the others is deafening now, and I deserve every word of it. I didn't protect Kyle when he was alive, I can't even avenge him now he's dead.

Useless.

Waste.

Of.

Space.

Then I look up. I can't believe how lucky I am because there they are, girl and bear, sitting by the door in a glitzy, shiny bubble of a shop – sniffing scented pens and chatting, with no sign of her interfering mother or bratty sister anywhere nearby. The adrenalin of the past few hours leaches away at the sight of her. The others are stunned into silence because they realise I was right about something for once. She *is* special – my chance to prove that I'm not the useless waste of space the others say I am. I will never let anyone hurt her. I will never let her down.

Chapter 23

Leah

I am holding the blades up, ready to strike, but my hands are shaking too much. Hot with shame, I realise I can't bring myself to do it.

I put the scissors down for a moment, give myself a hard stare in the gold-edged B&B mirror. *Come on you idiot, it's only hair.*

But it's not. In the days after it happened, Dad forgot to brush my hair. It didn't even occur to him until the tangles at the back behind my neck started to turn into a matted lump. I tried to get it out myself and Dad stumbled into my bedroom only to find me crying and tugging weakly at it with a brush.

The tangle was so bad by then that he had to snip it away, and after that he learned to deal with it. At first, he brushed too gently as if snagging my hair would unravel the whole gnarled tangle of pain in my head and pull his daughter apart, but as his confidence grew, he became better at it. We would sit together every morning and he would stroke Mum's old Mason Pearson brush firmly down my hair exactly one hundred times, his hand holding my shoulder gently, my body swaying with the rhythm of each brush stroke. Silence. We never spoke but the ritual helped me relax. I continued to let him do it well into my early teens for the comfort it brought us both.

Back then my hair was yellow gold, the perfect angelic colour for a media love affair, and even though it's darkened it is still part of my so-called public image. It's called Missing White Woman Syndrome – the blonder, the prettier and the more middle class you are, the more public sympathy you get – or at least the more media coverage. The hair is what people recognise. In the eyes of the world and in Dad's eyes, it's what makes me *me*.

If I cut it, I won't be as recognisable, I won't draw any undue attention. If Dad calls the police when he finds me gone – and it's likely he will, even if Ellie blabs about where I am – then looking different will give me a little more time before the word gets out.

And besides, I've always wondered what it would be like to cut it – just slice through that thick mane and chop it off at one stroke.

But the moment it comes off there's no going back. No pretending I'd just needed a bit of time to myself after the family row – *oops sorry, I forgot to leave a note*. No going back to hiding in my hole, making fundraising speeches, plodding through the school gates with all the other blurs, studying to get the grades for a degree I don't really want to do. No future wedding in someone else's dress followed by a safely suburban life. One slice of the scissors and I will become a different person. Not a saint, not a victim, but someone else – a new, unknown person. It feels like freedom – but the kind of freedom you get when you jump off a cliff.

I sink back onto the bed; the cheap mattress is so much harder than my beloved sagging one at home. The twin room is new and disappointing – sweaty, polyester-mix duvet covers, a pointless shiny satin cushion decorating each pillow. An attempt at a shabby-chic chest of drawers ruined by a missing handle. On the coaster next to me lies an undersized cup of coffee I made using all three sachets of Nescafé at once. I tell myself that's why I feel so dizzy but, really, it's the memories.

Over the years I've survived and clung onto the ribbons of my sanity by blocking out thoughts of that day, telling myself that I'm saving it up, converting it into anger and building the pressure until I have the perfect weapon to throw at my enemy. But since I made the decision to come here, I can't hold back the memories any more. They rise like a lethal wave and crash through my entire body, knocking everything else out of the way.

Grit sticking to my knees. Kentucky's fur in my hand, gripped tighter and tighter.

That little blue shoe.

Afterwards I told the police everything and nothing. They made it easy as they went to such lengths to protect me, the little victim. My story was drawn out of me through art therapy and gentle questions. I responded with the facts, the exact order in which things happened. The only time I wavered was when they asked if I had heard him coming.

'No, I didn't.' As I spoke, I could feel the whole story building up in my mind – the truth pushing at me, trying to escape.

'I was . . . distracted,' was all I could say before the sobs came.

If they had pushed me then I would have told them everything, but instead they paused the interview, gave me a plastic cup of water to help me recover. As I sipped, I tried to imagine how Dad would feel if he knew the truth: disgust, horror, anger. Would he hate me, push me away? What little life I had would crumble into nothing.

When the interview resumed the officer skipped forward, asked me to describe getting into the car, and my chance, my one and only chance to take responsibility had passed.

I told them I'd climbed onto my booster seat myself, that Mum was on the other side of the car strapping Carey in when it happened.

I saw movement out of the corner of my eye, light coming into the car where Mum had been pushed back. No screams, instead a gasp from her, a little noise of disbelief as she transformed from stressed but capable parent, to a terrified victim fighting to survive. As she realised that this was the end of everything. There was a soft sound as she slithered to the floor, which made me look up – and then his face, leaning into the car, looking at my sister. The knife slick in his hand. It happened too quickly for me to even breathe.

Carey cried out once. Carey, the girl full of noise and light, the girl who never stopped talking, who I told to shut up a thousand times a day. She cried out once.

Instinct kicked in. I slithered out of my seat into the footwell of the car – shivering, shuddering there among the empty juice boxes and lost Lego. I curled up and closed my eyes tighter,

tighter, burying my face in Kentucky's fur. *It was just a game. Just my imagination. Another monster from inside my head.*

I opened my eyes, looked up. Carey was still in her seat – her chubby legs sticking out and completely still – one blue shoe off and one still on.

I didn't tell the police what came next. Or any other living soul.

I stayed like that, eyes shut, not willing to make it real by opening them again. When I did, my friend was gone from Carey's side of the car. For a moment I thought he had run away, but then I felt him behind me, watching me through my open car door. A tiny, primal part of my seven-year-old mind told me that it was my turn, that I should run and hide, but scrambling to the other side of the car would mean passing under Carey's feet, and I just couldn't. There was nowhere to go.

I turned slowly, eyes blurred with little pinpricks of light dancing in my vision.

He was crouched down at my level, looking at me. His face shone, open and friendly the same way it always had – caterpillar eyebrows raised in questioning.

And then he spoke.

'I did this for you.'

It takes all my effort to rein my memories back in. I'm not going there. I'm never going there again. Instead I slip my hand into the ancient, battered suitcase and take out the knife, my fingers closing around the grip as I test its weight. I don't hold it for long. I just place it gently on my bedside, ready for later, like Ellie laying out her accessories on her dressing table the night before she's due to wear them.

Then I pick it up again and re-wrap it in the shirt. I don't want to look at it right now.

I fidget some more, tidying up the coffee cup and the empty Nescafé sachets.

Focus, Leah. You're cutting your hair, remember?

I put the wrapped-up knife in the shabby-chic bedside drawer and pull my hair into a loose ponytail at the back of my head.

In films – I have seen *some* films, you know – the hair always comes away in one clean, satisfying chop but mine is particularly stubborn. After several slices I still haven't cut through and tendrils have started to come loose, so I end up hacking through a thick uncontrollable mane until finally it's done. There is a ponytail in my hand, strands of cut-off hair stuck to the skin on my shoulders, and I now have a kind of bob. My head feels light, my neck cool and fresh. I like it.

Wrapping the ponytail in a tissue, I place it reverently in the bedside drawer next to the knife. I have vague ideas of donating it to a wig charity, but then I realise that after today my life as I know it will be blown to smithereens. I will not be researching hair charities, buying padded envelopes and popping down to the Post Office. I stuff it in the bin. I have done enough for good causes.

A movement in the corner of the room makes me look up and I see her, the girl in the mirror looking ordinary and a little bit sharp. My eyes look smaller somehow and I'm as pale as only someone who lives behind a bookcase can be. I notice that I'm not actually as beautiful as everyone says I am. It turns out it *was* all about the hair after all.

Chapter 24

Ellie

My heart was still thudding against my ribcage long after I'd got off the train at Waterloo station. I sat down on my case, my back leaning against a marble pillar, to catch my breath. The station was quiet – about as quiet as a London station ever gets. A straggled bunch of women on a hen do were slumped over by the clock – pink tutus reduced to rags and tiaras on sideways – not talking, just staring at their phones. Families with young kids moved steadily past them – off to the Natural History Museum or other wholesome educational places. Boring as their day was going to be, I would rather be them than me. Wafts of fake baking smells lured me towards a nearby coffee shop and I splurged a fiver on a reheated egg and bacon baguette. As I gnawed through it, cutting the roof of my mouth on the crust, I thumbed my way through the train route options on my phone. The price of the ticket almost made me spit out the baguette in horror; luckily Mum had slipped me some random money after the Amazing Children Awards to make me feel better about the row.

I had got this far on sheer panic alone, not letting myself think too much about what I was doing, but now, one by one I ran through the different possibilities of how this could play out. As I listed each one, a hard knot of dread grew tighter and tighter in my stomach.

Scenario One: Leah somehow tracks Crow down on the housing estate Pete mentioned. She confronts him and tells him how his actions have destroyed her life. Crow is truly sorry for what he did. He asks for forgiveness, and Leah feels an amazing sense of closure and goes home to her loving dad.

That one was not going to happen.

Scenario Two: Leah confronts Crow and turns out to be a secret ninja. Even though he is a hardened criminal, raised on one of the roughest estates in London, he is somehow floored by a girl who grew up in a bookshop. She beats him to a pulp and goes to jail, which ruins her life, David's life, Mum's life and – let's face it – mine.

That one was slightly more likely, but not much.

Scenario Three: Leah has a gun and shoots him from a distance.

No, that wasn't even possible – where on earth would Leah get a gun?

Scenario Four: Leah confronts Crow, he overpowers her easily then beats the shit out of her because he's an ex-gang member with a history of violent mental illness and some pretty serious demons.

This one was all too possible – it could even be far worse.

And I was going to stop it. Me. I let out a small yip of panicked laughter. The only person standing between Leah and Scenario Four was a vlogger with a slightly chipped sparkly manicure.

What the fucking hell was I doing?

Fuckfuckfuckfuck.

I said that last part out loud, prompting an evil look from a passing mama and her brood.

Of course, there was Scenario Five – one I'd rather not think about. What would Leah do to me if I got in her way? She hated me, she'd made that pretty clear over the last year or so. So why on earth would she listen to me? I grabbed my phone and brought up David's number, my finger hesitating over the call icon. Then I thought about his irrational levels of protectiveness, how Leah never seemed to notice his face crumble every time she even frowned slightly. I thought about Mum, flailing uselessly back and forth between me and David, not knowing what to do about my vlog. I thought about Dad dropping everything and running off to Australia with someone new as if you can just neatly leave one life behind and slot into another. And I realised that parents really can't solve anything. They're just as clueless as we are – in fact sometimes they're worse as they don't realise how little they know. David's protectiveness had sealed Leah in a see-through bubble, cushioning her from the outside world so much that she was unable ever really to touch it. He didn't have a clue what was really going on in her head. He'd been messing things up for years – how could he possibly get it right now?

I had to find her before it all happened. Assuming she'd snuck out of the shop last night and got the latest train, she had a whole ten hours' head start on me and I had no idea where she was going. The only advantage was that she didn't really know either. I guessed her plan was to ask around the estate until she found Sam Clarke, then try to get him alone, to do whatever it was she thought she could do. Had she even thought about what would happen next?

It was then I remembered my laptop – it had been in the 'family room' all night and when I went to get it this morning the power light was blinking on, so I knew somebody had used it. It could have been Leah.

Baguette in hand, dragging my case behind me, I ran back into the coffee shop hoping to see . . . *Yes*. A sign saying FREE WI-FI.

Ten minutes later I was haring down the platform, feet thundering on the shiny floor, case flying out behind me, its crooked wheel making it bounce and jump around my ankles. I threw it between the doors and myself straight after it, just as they closed. I'd made it.

I knew where she was going – her internet history had shown me a nondescript B&B near the station that she'd looked at on more than one travel site. But apart from that her history was all schoolwork related and I had no idea what she was planning to do. My hands started shaking again as the train pulled out of the station, creaking and groaning into the grey, drizzly morning light. Opposite me, a man sat staring down at his lap. He was wearing a suit, but his tie had long gone and there was a can of Strongbow on the table between us, a sour smell coming off his body. A woman lowered herself into the seat next to me with a gentle sigh and a waft of Coco Mademoiselle. She slapped a pile of magazines on the table and proceeded to flick through them with fat, pink shellacked fingers. Squirming in my seat I got my phone out of my back pocket. I couldn't face Instagram or Snapchat, and ignored my WhatsApp messages which were probably about the party I'd missed last night. That wasn't my life any more.

I had two hours to kill before I risked my life to save the stepsister who hated me, and nothing else to do but play Bubble Quest and stare out of the window.

Chapter 25

Leah

Never in my entire sheltered life have I walked into a pub by myself and struck up a conversation with a complete stranger, but by my third one I was kind of used to it. And this one wasn't one of those gastro pubs which makes its money selling oversized pies or a family-friendly place with a climbing frame in the garden outside. This pub garden is a stubbly grass verge about three metres long peppered with fag ends, stained beer mats and broken glass. The facade is grey concrete, made even greyer by the fine drizzle that is also forming beads of moisture in my hair and coating everything in icy wetness. Above the door, a shabby, faded sign shows a picture of a yacht, the word picked out in peeling gold paint. I step over a full nappy sack to get inside.

It's dark – the only light comes from the thin, high-up windows and a flickering row of fruit machines lined up against the far wall. The lights aren't on either. Maybe it messes with the clientele's hangovers.

Once my eyesight adjusts, I realise it's not so bad, provided that all you want to do in it is drink or play fruit machines. There's an old guy in the corner with a pint of stout and a copy of the *Sun* crossword in front of him. A brown dog is curled at his feet, its chin resting on his leg. A couple of other drinkers lurk in the shadows by the entrance to the gents' toilet – they don't look up when I come in.

I slope up to the bar, settling onto a stool as the barman walks over. I order a vodka and Coke, because this looks like the kind of place that won't card you. I'm right, he doesn't, but I do get a raised eyebrow. I blush hot and red, as I feel my sheltered middle-classness coming off me in waves. It doesn't matter that I've cut my hair and put make-up on my face, or that I'm wearing one of Ellie's cheap fake leather jackets, I am still me and I have no idea what I am doing.

No, I tell myself. *You know exactly what you're doing. Pull yourself together.* If this makes me uncomfortable, how the hell am I going to do what's coming next?

I switch on the coldness, the calculating mode that I use to read people when I'm out in the world. I size up the situation. The barman is middle-aged, black, shaven headed with a warm friendly face. He needs a couple of minutes to get used to me but once he does, he's going to get curious. I take a sip of my drink and try not to react as the vodka hits the back of my throat.

'Are you sure you want that?' the barman asks, and I give myself bonus points for my people-reading skills.

'Hair of the dog,' I say, smiling. 'I was at a party last night, haven't really been to sleep.'

He nods – the bags under my eyes back up the story. His body language relaxes – shoulders down, smile loosening and becoming more genuine. His neat, angular beard changes shape as he adjusts his expression and leans on the bar. I revise my assessment of him from *Nice Bloke* to *Nice Bloke but thinks he's a bit of a player.*

This makes me nervous. I don't know how to handle that kind of thing. I don't do flirting. For a couple of moments, the plan flies out of my head, I can't think. I make a misstep. I know I'm pushing the wrong button even as the words leave my mouth but it's too late to stop them.

'I met a guy last night, really liked him, but I lost his number, can you believe it? He's called Sam something. Sam . . . um . . . Clarke?'

The shutters slam down on the player's face. He pushes back off the bar, turns his back and starts stacking glasses.

'Fuck me, you lot look younger all the time,' he says with a rueful little laugh. 'What are you, just out of journalism school or something?'

I stutter something about not being a journalist, that he's got it wrong. He just shakes his head. I take another sip of the drink and can almost feel the vodka making its way into my bloodstream, hot and invigorating.

'I can pay you,' I say.

He just laughs. 'Look, I don't know what this bloke has or hasn't done or why you people are so interested in finding him, but I've been running this pub for the last five years and there's only one rule I stick to: I don't get involved. I think you need to leave, Lois Lane.'

Outside, the sun has broken through the clouds, glaring off the inky-black puddles on the pavement. I'm blinking, partly from the dazzling effect and partly from the feeling of downing a whole vodka in two minutes flat. Tears are streaming from my eyes.

What a joke I am. What a sad little sheltered, privileged, weakling joke. *Mum, Carey, I can't do it. I've let you down.*

I'm rummaging in my pockets for a tissue when I sense someone standing next to me and look up. It's a woman, dyed red hair growing out into streaks of grey, pulled high into a pony-tail away from a weathered, lined face and sharp grey eyes. Her ears are heavily pierced – rows and rows of silver charms of all different shapes and sizes hang from them, like she's carrying her life story around with her. For a moment I think she's going to comfort me or ask me what's wrong.

'How much exactly?' she says in a voice heavy with fags and drink.

It takes me a moment to reply – I'm hot with shame at being caught like this, vulnerable as an open wound. I don't trust my voice not to croak when I speak.

'Fifty,' I finally manage.

'Seventy-five. No address but I know where he hangs around, you'll be able to find him.'

I nod, and use those few moments to get myself together, let the coldness settle on me again. I have money rolled up in my jeans pocket. Part of me panics at getting it out in front of her – will she just take it all from me without giving me the information? What if she just makes something up? I am completely, utterly in her power.

I give her fifty, hold the rest in my hand until she gives me the information I need. She looks at me long and hard, as if trying to figure out who I am, why Sam Clarke is so interesting. The silver teddy bear dangling from the bottom of her left ear trembles slightly, looking forlorn.

'There's a party tonight – Jayden's place in Bevan House. He fixed Jay's bike up for him last week, so he'll probably be there. Fourth floor, you won't miss it – too fucking loud!' Her laugh is dry and cracked.

She explains where the party is, and I hand her thirty pounds as I don't have a five-pound note. I try to leave as gracefully as I can but my heart is hammering.

This is real.

I don't know what to do now, where to go. I walk the streets for a couple of hours, wander through the shops, staring at cheap shiny clothes which mean nothing to me. Inside I feel light – there's a kind of excitement bubbling up as if I'm about to head off on an adventure. I walk down to the beach but the wind hits me hard, chilling me to the bone under the flimsy pleather jacket until I run back up the hill to the station and to the B&B.

As I approach, I notice a figure sitting on the steps. A girl, legs propped on a glittery pink wheelie suitcase, one knee showing through her artfully ripped jeans, fiddling with her phone. As I get closer, I notice something familiar about her and then my heart stops.

Ellie. Bloody Ellie.

I spin on my heels, start walking away down the street, but it's too late. She's seen me.

Chapter 26

Ellie

My legs were stiff and sore from sitting as I jumped up and sprang down the hill after her. I hadn't recognised her for a second with the hatchet job she'd done on her hair. It was browner without the long ends bleached by the sun and the effect made her face seem paler. She looked like she hadn't slept. As I caught up with her, I grabbed her sleeve and she looked at me, eyes wide with panic. I realised I'd broken that No Touching Leah Stoke rule again.

I'd had a speech prepared, on the train down. Something worthy of a Hollywood movie, a speech that would not only stop Leah in her tracks but make her stand up and applaud at the end. It was only now that I was about to say it, I realised it was a ridiculous pile of crap.

I was still working out what to say when Leah started looking frantically around her. 'Where is he?' she said. 'I can't let him see me.'

For a minute I thought she was talking about Crow, and then I realised. She honestly thought I'd brought David down with me.

'He's not here,' I said. 'I didn't tell him. I came by myself.'

I felt her arm relax under my grip and I let go of her – I couldn't exactly stop her going anywhere. Suddenly she was laughing – genuine peals of laughter. Her whole expression changed to one of relief.

She made me a tiny cup of weak tea using the little kettle in her room. She offered me a biscuit as I shifted uncomfortably on one of the twin beds. I found myself scrabbling around in my head for small talk – anything to avoid discussing why I was really there. At one point I suggested she tried colouring her hair blue. Seriously.

She laughed again – she'd laughed pretty much constantly since I'd arrived, as if I'd unplugged something inside her. She seemed different now she was away from the shop, freer somehow.

I began to hope that everything was going to be all right, that somehow my turning up had stopped her from finding Crow, or that maybe she'd found it too difficult and given up on the idea. Fleetingly, I thought we might enjoy the seaside for a few hours – a walk on the seafront, a go on the slot machines, some fish and chips before heading home to a grateful David and Mum. *Well done Ellie, you saved the day!*

'I'm not sure,' Leah said, peering in the mirror and running her fingers through her hair. 'I wouldn't mind red. Or maybe I'll just grow it again.'

'No,' I said. 'You look better, more grown up and less like you live in a cupboard in a shop. The leather jacket doesn't suit you, though.'

'It wasn't meant to – it's supposed to be a disguise.'

And there we were again, slap bang back on the doorstep of the reason why we were both here.

We both spoke at the same time. I started my impassioned speech just as she said, 'There's nothing you can do to stop me, you know.'

'Don't you care what will happen to you afterwards?' I asked.

Leah threw her head back and gave another little peal of laughter. 'Oh, Ellie, what do you think I'm going to do? I only want to talk to him.'

Her words sent a flood of relief flowing through me – I mean what she was planning to do was still dangerous and half mad, but at least she wasn't going to try and beat him up. I started laughing too at the ridiculousness of the idea.

Leah explained that a few years ago David had received a letter from Crow's lawyer offering a meeting. 'Restorative justice, it's called,' Leah said. 'We get a chance to meet up and ask him questions – he gets a chance to say sorry. But Dad didn't want that – he decided I wasn't ready for it. But I am. I need to see him, Ellie.'

She explained her plan, this party he was supposed to be going to.

'I hate to sound like your dad, but that doesn't sound especially safe,' I said, cringing at the parental tone in my voice.

'It's my only lead,' she told me. 'I tramped around all morning asking people and this party is the only clue I've got. If he's drunk or he's taken drugs I'll keep my distance. I'm not stupid, Ellie.'

No, she wasn't stupid, but had she ever actually seen someone on drugs? Probably not. Oh. Apart from that one time, that one person.

'I'm going with you,' I said. 'Now, how much money have you got?'

'A bit, why?'

'There are two ways to get into a party when you're not invited. The first one is to dress uber-sexy – I don't fancy that option, do you? The second is to bring shitloads of booze.'

The Attlee estate would probably have been nice when it was new. It wasn't a forest of grey concrete tower blocks – it was built of brown brick and each flat had a lovely wide-open balcony on one side and a friendly terraced walkway on the other. There were trees and green open spaces so people could hang out and chat with their neighbours. There was a play park for the kiddies with bright red and yellow tubular metal things to climb on.

But up close the park was sad and shabby. All the climbing frames were scuffed and damaged, the kids had long since gone home and now the park was empty, save for a bunch of teens hanging on the swings and drinking WKD in the half-light of dusk. Walking across the lawn, we found it was just a gnarled tangle of dried mud and weeds, with crisp packets and polystyrene takeaway containers ground into the dirt. A not-very-talented street artist had been at the walls of Bevan House: just next to the stairwell entrance someone had drawn a huge cock and balls in yellow spray paint.

'Oh, so *that's* Banksy,' Leah said as we went past, into the darkness. My fingers were already sore from the carrier bag full of cheap spirits, clanking together as we climbed the stairs.

The stairwell did not smell of piss, as I'd been half expecting. Instead there was a rotten, sweet stench that made my stomach turn over – it smelled like the time Mum had found a dead pigeon in the yard behind the bookshop.

At the top of the first flight of stairs we found what it was – an ancient roast chicken carcass just lying there on a step, bones jutting through the skin, flakes of white flesh scattered across the landing. I held my free hand up to my mouth, breathing through my sleeve. The scent of Mum's favourite fabric conditioner hit me even harder. *Flowers of the Forest. Home.*

The soft doof-doof of the bass led us up the stairs, and as the smell cleared the sound filled the air, squeezing out all the other senses until all we could do was listen. By the third floor I could feel it through my feet, so I knew this had to be the right place. Up until then I'd half hoped we'd be turned away at the door, but I knew then, with a feeling of sinking desperation, that it wasn't going to happen. When you throw a house party this loud, you have to invite the whole neighbourhood. We walked straight in.

There was something immediate, desperate about the party – as if they knew that music this loud couldn't last long before the cops were called. Blinds shut against the dregs of the day, rooms clogged with smoke and weed, carpet already sticky underfoot. It took my eyes a couple of moments to adjust and then I could see the faces – people drinking, dancing, even though it wasn't dark yet. The parties I had been to before were so different – girls and boys pushed together for a couple of hours of deliberate fun which only livened up when everyone was drunk enough. This party was fluid, organic, like it had a life of its own. That's when I realised that a good party, a really good one, has to be a little bit scary.

Leah said something to me. I leaned closer, lifting my hair away from my ear – as if that would help. 'WHERE IS HE?'

I shrugged, yelled something about acting natural and wove my way through to where I thought the kitchen might be, eager to dump the heavy bottles. The music was just as loud in here – a huge speaker on the kitchen worktop looped into the rest. This was where the serious drinkers were, propped up against the chipped worktops – one actually sitting in the sink, skinny legs in ripped jeans dangling over the side. I waggled a bottle of JD in their direction and they gave a happy cheer. Turning to Leah, I pressed a beer can into her hand and cracked one open myself, drinking a sip too fast and getting a mouthful of froth. Leah took a gulp and her face twisted in disgust.

'KEEP DRINKING. WE NEED TO BLEND IN,' I said. I had already decided to leave it ten minutes and then somehow get her out of here, persuade her to come home. *At least we tried*, I'd tell her.

But in the meantime, what? We couldn't talk, couldn't even think – the music had flooded into my brain and there was no room for anything else. All we could do was either drink or dance, so I tried to do both.

Back in the lounge the battered leather sofa and chairs had been pushed back against the walls, full of draped people nursing beer cans, yelling in each other's ears or just staring comfortably into space. In the centre of the room, about a dozen people were dancing. I just dived in and joined them.

After a few moments I forgot the time of day, forgot I was still sober and why we were there, and just let myself move. I looked around for Leah, expecting to see her leaning against a wall, tut-tutting at frivolous little me, but she was gone.

Shit. Shit. Shit.

I spun around, spilling beer and not caring, my heart hammering in panic.

'LEAH!' I shouted pointlessly, whirling once again, desperate.

Then a hand, tapping my shoulder. Leah, rolling her eyes at me. I had looked all around the room for her, in the dark corners and on the sofa but I hadn't looked among the dancers, hadn't even imagined she would be there. But now she was, her body swaying, dancing with some guy. And she was smiling.

Chapter 27

Leah

I hate this music. This mindless thumping, hitting me over the head with endless bass, but it's in my body and every cell in me is jumping to it. My shoulders start to sway, my feet move without me telling them to. Hot, I slip out of the fake leather jacket and kick it to one side. A guy in a white T-shirt with tight muscles and a stubbly grin spots me. *Come on*, I see him mouth as he reaches out. *Dance with me*. There is a tattoo of a snake – its head in the crook of his thumb, its black scaled body coiling and undulating up the man's arm, rippling as he moves. I follow the serpent.

I like this man – I like his smile, his confidence, the way he looks at me, which is three parts lust and one part curiosity. As I dance, I raise my bare arms in the air and it lifts something in me. The rest of my body sways, my face is tight from smiling. Nobody is staring at me, monitoring my well-being or wondering what is going on in my head, what this crazy dancing means. Am I happy? Am I sad? Do I need extra support at this critical time? I am nobody. I am Woman On Dance Floor, an extra in somebody else's movie.

The man puts his hands on my hips. This is moving fast for me but I let him keep them there a few moments – there's a warm, melting feeling in my skin where his hands are pressing against me. The warmth spreads slowly across my back, down between my thighs, like sinking into a hot bath. It makes me feel real, solid. I want him to move his hands to the small of my back, pull me closer. I want to know how it feels to lean into his body and feel his torso press against mine. I want to stroke his close-cropped hair, his rough chin, study the contours of his face and then kiss him.

But then what? I am not ready to lose control completely, I can't. It takes a lot of effort to pull back. I give him a smile which I hope means no hard feelings. And I keep dancing.

How do people do it? How do they just let go like this, open themselves up to different experiences, let new people in? It seems to come easily to Ellie – a room full of people is like an undiscovered country to her; she's off exploring before she's even had a chance to think. Or is she faking it too, pretending to be this chirpy, confident thing to further her own plans? Maybe everyone has a cold centre like mine.

Suddenly the air inside the flat is too hot, the girl dancing next to me pokes me with her elbow yet again. *Is she trying to force me away?* After a few moments my snake-man moves away to dance with a group of people, and I feel awkward again. I put my arms down, back away from the crowd.

Outside on the balcony, a row of smokers stare out across the estate – their eyes trained on the dark horizon, their arms leaning on the wall with lit cigarettes dangling from between their fingers. A girl with green braids offers me one and I take it. I've only ever smoked that one with Ellie but when I take my first draw there's a sense of comfort, of recognition. I'm obviously a natural smoker, which is annoying as I don't like weaknesses. The group is talking about people and places I don't know, but I don't feel awkward standing on the edge – the cigarette shields me somehow.

I use the time to think, away from Ellie's gaze. It was so easy to convince her that I meant Crow no harm. She's spent her entire life being cared for, meeting nice people who feel guilty if they so much as trap a mouse. The idea that someone – a well brought-up, sheltered little girly like me – could even think about being violent to someone seems crazy to her.

As the cigarette wears down, I make my move.

'My friend didn't turn up,' I say to green braids girl. 'Sam Clarke? He's supposed to be here but I can't find him.'

She looks at me blankly when I say Crow's fake name but her boyfriend, one protective arm around her, knows who I'm talking about. He thinks it's funny, that I've been stood up. I feel a wave of nausea at the idea.

'No, it's not that . . . He was going to fix my bike up for me. He does that, you know. Fixes bikes?'

Look at me: Friend Of Sam, knowing all about his life.

They can't help me, but I have my story straight now. And a flat full of people. Someone is bound to know where Crow is.

Chapter 28

Ellie

'FORKLIFT!'

Turns out that word is hilariously funny wherever you say it! I got bored with the beer and went onto the Jack Daniel's, pouring some into a Finding Dory paper cup I found in the kitchen, along with a splash of Coke. Funnily enough, about twenty minutes after I'd downed it the party became absolutely amazing.

So I had another couple, and they felt pretty good too. And I might have taken something, I didn't quite remember.

I danced, and when I got tired of dancing I yell-chatted. The people here were funny and brilliant and different, and had been through loads of eye-popping shit which they were all too eager to tell me about.

There was this guy, Guy. No seriously! I know! Anyway, Guy was lovely and camp and super funny, and gave me all the gossip on everyone in the room. And I told him how I just love going to gay bars because I don't have to worry about being perved over by straight cisgender men. Guy didn't seem too impressed by that, but he had this wickedly bitchy story about the time he'd snogged a celebrity, which took our minds completely off the awkward moment. I wondered if I could take Guy home with me and make him my friend.

I hadn't forgotten why I was there, though, not at all. Every now and then I'd glance over to the door of the flat and see Leah standing there, leaning moodily against the balcony and chain-smoking. Did she know she was talking to the party's official drug dealer? Probably best not to tell her. I giggled.

Just then the speakers blared out the first notes of my favourite track – my must-dance anthem. I wished Billie and Gloria were here to dance with me. But then I had Guy, and he was dancing too. And then I had a flash of inspiration – diving down the side of the ratty sofa I found my bag nestled in with everyone else's and rummaged around until, at the bottom with all the biscuit crumbs and paperclips, I found my last tube of glitter. I scrambled up onto the sofa arm to throw it out into the crowd.

Guy was going to *love* this.

'FORKLIFT!'

I shook the tube out as hard as I could and glitter flew across the room, landing on the crusty guy on the sofa, the dancing girls in their tiny bodycon dresses, the sexy snake tattoo man, and Guy.

For an agonising millisecond everyone looked up, confused, but then Guy laughed and as one, the crowd reached into the air, grabbing at the glitter as it stuck to their arms, their hair, glinting in the flashing LED lights. It was so beautiful.

Then Guy reached up and lifted me – off the sofa cushions, over everyone's heads. I reached out with my arms just like that girl in *Dirty Dancing*. I flew like that for a few amazing micro-seconds, looking down at the glitter-struck room, my head pounding with the music. And then I felt his arms begin to tremble before he slowly lowered me down.

'You're crazy, you are.'

'I know,' I said proudly.

I wondered what Leah was thinking. It must have been weird for her, being at a party with other humans.

She wasn't over by the drug dealer any more, and she wasn't dancing.

My heart began to flutter in my chest. Not full-blown panic, just a nagging worry. I told myself to stay calm – after all, I thought I'd lost her before. I checked in the kitchen, in the queue for the bathroom and – after knocking loudly and coughing elaborately – in the bedrooms. Nothing.

I burst back into the living room – the LED lights were flashing on a super-fast setting now, turning each flying speck of glitter into a tiny laser beam, dazzling and dizzying amid the flailing limbs of the dancers. Pushing through the tangle of bodies I shouted her name as loudly as I could. Nobody could hear me.

Now my heart was thudding, head dizzy with panic. I saw Guy, grabbed his elbow.

'HAVE YOU SEEN MY FRIEND?'

'The sulky-looking blonde? Wasn't she talking to Chas out front?'

I looked towards the door again. The dealer was gone too. *Oh shit, she's gone off with a drug dealer. David will kill me, slowly and painfully.*

But worse – what if she'd found Crow and gone off with him?

I ran from person to person, shaking them, asking them if they knew somebody called Crow. People were too out of it to care, too freaked out by the mad-eyed, staring glitter-bomber asking the questions.

Grabbing my bag, I struggled through the crowd to the front door, past the smokers on the walkway and down to the dimly lit staircase. As the music receded, I started to feel normal again, sober. I managed to catch a bus back to the B&B. Leah had the key, but luckily the landlady was there to let me in.

My ears rang in the silence of the room. I kicked off my shoes, picked a bed – the one that Leah hadn't already slept in – and climbed under the duvet. Not so I could sleep, but just so I had somewhere warm and comfortable to think.

Leah was missing, last seen talking to a dealer at a drug-fuelled house party while trying to trace a notorious, mentally disturbed killer. I should call the police now.

And yet if I did, how the hell could I explain all this without getting Leah into trouble?

Because I realised now that Leah had lied to me about just wanting to talk. At ten years old Leah had wanted to hurt Crow. She had written about it, prayed about it, researched it – how could I have forgotten the hard scratch of her childish handwriting, the smears of red felt tip pen on the page? Maybe most normal people wouldn't be capable of taking things this far, but Leah wasn't normal – she hadn't stood a chance of being normal after what happened to her.

And then there was me. The absolute, complete prize fuck-up that was me. I'd gone with Leah to the party to look out for her, and what had I done? Performed. Thrown glitter. Found a fabulous bloke to bond with. Got pissed. Everything David had said about me was right.

These thoughts went round and round in my head, butting against each other until the light in the room went from streetlight-yellow to grey and a steady rain began to fall, splashing against the window pane. Fuck. It was morning and I still hadn't done anything.

A scraping sound made me jump out of bed. A key in the door, a flood of relief and joy. *She was back, she was OK, we were OK . . .*

And then I saw the blood on her hands.

She stumbled towards me on shaky legs and when my horrified eyes met hers, she crumpled into my arms, her whole body trembling with the force of her sobs.

Chapter 29

Leah

I leave the party with an address written on my hand in shaky biro. The lock-up where Crow fixes mopeds. No more waiting, no more excuses. I find it on my maps app and head straight there on foot. I walk quickly and quietly, striding through the estate with an air of confidence backed up by four years' intensive training in mixed martial arts.

I'm not thinking about what I'm going to do. Not at all.

But even without conscious thought, the reality of it has seeped into my muscles and bones. As I get closer my hands begin to tremble, my legs turn to rubber and try to buckle with every stride. My chest feels tight and I realise my breathing is too frenzied, too fast. I reach into my training to try to rein it in, but my body won't listen, won't obey me.

It would be easy to sit down on a wall, take a few breaths and psych myself up again, but if I stop I'm not sure I'll have the strength to get up again. All I can do is trust my anger to get me through.

I think again about Carey, about her singing the same stupid nursery rhymes over and over, about her bashing me with her foot under the dinner table to wind me up then denying it to our parents. I think about the time we went away to that cottage with the pool, built an island out of floats tied together and lived as castaways for the afternoon. And I think about that little blue shoe, that one cry and the fear she must have felt.

There is such cold hatred in my heart, such rage.

I will end him.

The estate peters out towards the edge of town. The darkest part of the night is gone. The sun is not up yet but I can see a few pitiful rows of flats stretch out into a car park area littered with piles of fly-tipping – rotten mattresses, layers of damp, rain-soaked paper, old Lucozade bottles. On the edge of this is a semi-derelict industrial estate, full of boarded-up buildings. The rotted gates are open and look like they haven't moved in years. I make my way across the cracked forecourt to a small row of garages with rusted metal doors. One door is crumpled like waste paper, as if a car has rammed it head-on. Another two have tall grass and weeds pushing up through the pitted concrete in front of them – they look like nobody's been inside in years.

The fourth one is open into the near darkness. There's a light on inside, the tinny buzz of a cheap phone speaker playing R&B tracks. There's a half-dismantled Vespa in the centre of the garage, parts spilled out on the floor like blood and guts.

He is alone. He's sitting at a table on a battered old office chair, one wheel missing, foam pouring out of the stuffing. His skinny shoulders, clad in a faded black T-shirt, hunched over as he concentrates on whatever he's doing. An angle-poise lamp pools light around his head – a tragically misguided halo.

I'm shaking. Shaking. Shaking.

My feet are rooted to the spot. I can't move, my legs simply won't do it. This is madness, I don't stand a chance.

Remember the knife.

I step back and slide my trembling hand into my bag, to the knife. My hand closes around the rubberised grip of the handle and I feel my fingers slot into its grooves – slightly too large and far apart for a woman. As I grip it, some of my strength and resolve comes back. What was it the newspapers said? Nobody could possibly carry this knife without intend-ing to harm another human being. As I pull it out, it catches the light from the garage and gleams, like in a film. But this is real, and it's heavy in my hand.

I'm holding the knife low down by my side, in the outward position. *This is it. Shoulders relaxed.*

One soft step forward, sneakers treading gently on the stony tarmac. His shoulders remain unmoved.

Another step.

He's humming now: Rihanna. Murderers hum. Murderers listen to R&B. They fix motorcycles, they live, they breathe and laugh.

I know the best way to hurt him. I know I should rush at him, take him by surprise without a sound, but deep down I've always known that would be impossible. He has to know that it's me.

229

'Crow.' My voice creaks as if I haven't spoken in years.

At the sound of his old name he jumps up and spins to face me. The chair falls back with a clang onto the floor, small engine parts scatter off the table.

I see his face for the first time in ten years and it's a wreck. Hollow eyes, a tooth missing, and something else missing too, something invisible to the naked eye. He's not looking at me, not really, just scrabbling around in his mind looking for a way to react to the sound of his old name. I can see him considering denying it, throwing that thought away, and then slowly his lip curls, his shoulders set, and he plants his feet apart in a defensive stance. I see him pulling himself together, remembering who he was.

Not the pathetic troubled soul who went to jail, who got clean, did his time and did all those worthy prison activities. Not the young man who learned to read and write, fix mopeds, and made new friends. But Crow – who ran with gangs, who made deals, did messy jobs for the bigger boys. He beat people up, they said it in court. He knew where to hit, where to stab to cause the most damage. Even before he saw my family, he'd shed blood and hurt people. That's the man looking back at me now.

I grip the knife harder, while keeping it low and hidden in the semi-darkness.

Sometimes in my daydreams of this moment, he would know exactly who I was, he'd even laugh at me before the violence began. Other times, he would be a mess of a human being, grovelling at my feet. This real Crow watches me warily. There is no recognition on his face.

'Leah Stoke,' I say.

He swears softly, but I see another change in the way he's standing. His shoulders lose some of their tension, his face relaxes. He's relieved. Glad I'm not some gang member he's pissed off, some other more lethal face from his past. I am no threat to him.

'I read your dad's book,' he says.

What the fuck. We're going to have a fucking *conversation*?

I say nothing, keep my gaze on him and watch him flounder, but it's a mistake – he spots the knife.

He moves quickly, going for my arm. The knife clatters out of my hand but I move fast, blocking him, twisting his wrist. His phone slips out of his pocket and lands with a crack on the floor. I stamp on it and the music stops. Then I make my move, grappling him the way I brought down Bradley in MMA. I tip him off balance and his bulk crashes down on the cement floor, the air rushes from his lungs as he makes contact. I feel it, a repulsive blast of breath, a smell of coffee and cigarettes that makes him real to me, but I hold my focus, throw my weight on top of him. My mind is already two steps ahead. But then I feel the alignment of his body change under me. He's gathering strength and before I have a chance to react, he simply sits up and shoves me hard, nearly loosening my grip. I flip my legs around, trying to get his neck in a head scissor, but as I move, he lands a punch just under my ribs.

God it hurts. For a second all I can think about is the pain.

And then he has forced me down, holding my shoulder. I'm fighting, flailing, my mind working overtime on how to lever myself up again but I can feel myself tiring, my strength reserves are wearing down. I summon up a burst of strength and reach for the knife, but he kneels on my arm and another explosion of pain roars through my body. I am pinned under his weight like a beetle on its back.

He has hit me twice and I am almost destroyed. I realise that this is it, this is how my life will end. I'll never go home, never travel, never escape the shop, never become anything but Leah Stoke, who lived a victim and died a victim. I push back – *no, no, never* . . . But I have seen before that just wanting to live isn't enough when someone wants to kill you.

The feeling of helplessness tightens in my chest and bursts out of my mouth in a sob.

Then something changes. Crow's body shifts again; he pulls his weight off me and scrambles back, panting. He's just staring at me, his mouth open. It's then that I understand. He doesn't want to hurt me as much as I want to hurt him.

The knife is in my hand before I even have a chance to think about it. Adrenalin flushes through my body as I prepare to strike.

Then he speaks.

'You know, I used to talk to you, in the night after lights out,' he says. 'Just, like, a whisper. I thought if I kept talking, that somehow you might be able to hear me and that I could make you understand.'

I am stunned, my grip on the knife loosens but I'm barely aware of it. His eyes flicker down, away from me in shame. I want to press home my advantage – his legs are prone, hands resting on the ground. *A good stamp could break his fingers.* But I'm frozen by the sound of his voice, the same one from years ago when I trusted him. Now the question is there, bubbling up into my mouth. The one I asked myself time and time again, late at night in my room, staring at that crack in the ceiling. For a split second I couldn't bring myself to do it – the words have been locked in my head for so long I didn't know how to say them.

'Did you do it because of me?' I ask.

He is silent. For three seconds, four seconds, all I can hear is our breath. I'm so afraid of what he's going to say, but I have to hear it. I must know for sure.

'I just wanted to protect you, I wanted to keep you safe.'

I cannot move. The knife slithers from my limp fingers and I feel a wave of weakness crash over me.

I've always known it was my fault, that Mum and Carey are gone because of my anger, pride and stubbornness, but it's not the same as hearing the words, the final confirmation. *I am a killer. I am a killer.*

Crow is curled up now, sobbing out his own grief, as if it has any comparison to mine. *This is my chance – get in quick and low, stab and twist.*

Yes, that's what I need to do next, and then I deserve every bit of the punishment that follows. Only I'm not doing it – I'm turning on my heels, running, grabbing the garage door and slamming it shut. There's an open padlock in the latch and my fingers fumble as I grab it, suddenly so cold against the chilly metal. Time slows. I fumble again. Inside, Crow kicks at the metal, making a sound like thunder.

Click. The lock is in place and I'm running again. My feet slamming down on the asphalt so fast, out of control. I can feel every stone through the soles of my shoes. My legs are pumping, in pain but full of life, my lungs are filled with air, even my arm has stopped hurting. As I run, I feel something soaring, a joy disconnected from anything I've said or done – the result of simply running and being alive.

When I stop, I have no idea where I am – a part of the estate built out of dull brown brick, a stubbly green lawn with old washing lines on it, strung from concrete posts. I lean into one of the posts like it's Dad, hugging it. I am crying now, the euphoria has gone and I know I've failed.

Carey, Mum, I'm so sorry.

Without thinking I push back against the post and slam my fists into it – one-two, one-two, until the pain kicks in and forces me to feel something other than utter worthlessness.

Chapter 30

Ellie and Leah

Ellie

Leah wept in my arms for a long time. I stayed there, locked in the hug, scared to move and afraid to break the momentum of her tears. *What have you done, Leah? What have you done?* The question pulsed in my head but I couldn't bring myself to ask.

Slowly her breath slowed. I felt her shoulders stiffen as she became herself again, and realised she was hugging the Glitter Queen. I loosened my arms to allow her to pull away when she was ready, but she lingered just a fraction of a second longer – probably because she knew that as soon as she broke free, she would have to speak.

As she drew back, I saw the knuckles of her hands were scratched and bruised. She held them like two claws and blood was oozing from the cuts.

'We need to get you some ice,' I said.

A pointless statement as there wasn't even a mini fridge in the room. I led Leah to the bathroom and ran her hands under the cold tap, gently brushing the grit away and watching the water run pink down the drain. She just went along with it, floppy as a ragdoll, as I soaked her nightshirt and wrapped it gently around her hands.

And there, as she perched on the edge of the bath, the bundle of her hands limp in her lap, with the water soaking through her jeans, she began to speak.

She talked about a little girl forced into being a hero, told that she had to forgive and that her anger was wrong. About the guilt of waking up each morning in a bright pink bedroom surrounded by all the toys you'd ever want, and knowing that your sister would never steal any of them because you were the lucky one and she wasn't. About how impossible it is to forget, even for a minute, and how you struggle and muddle through day-to-day life when your mother and sister's death has become your father's full-time job. And she spoke about how it was all her fault.

'Leah, it's really not.' I finally broke the spell after listening in silence. 'It isn't. Everyone says it, you were just in the wrong place at the wrong time.'

Those words made her flinch. She shook her head, the blunt edges of her hair brushing her cheeks. Her eyes were pink rimmed and screwed shut – she'd been talking through a blur of tears for over an hour now, but she still had more to say.

Leah

When I was little, I used to like funny words. Bibliophile, Association, Affirmative. Dad thought it was funny to hear long words from a toddler's mouth, so he'd bring me more of them and give them to me like presents. At school it was just one of the things which made me different from other children – I never really fitted in, even before I became the class tragedy freak. When I was five a concerned teacher told my parents that she was worried that I didn't play well with others. I preferred creating my own imaginary world in a corner of the playground by myself, and if someone came up to join in, I'd tell them to go away. I remember them talking to me about this – Mum seemed worried, but Dad seemed proud. He told me not to worry, to go my own way. I was smarter than the other kids, anyway.

I wasn't bothered about friends from school, not when I had my family, but there must have been something missing, because otherwise Kentucky would never have existed.

We were at the fair the summer before Carey was born. Mum's belly was huge – she was changing in ways I didn't understand and I was uneasy about it. I can still remember the shooting gallery now – the battered tin cans, Mum squinting down the sights of her BB gun, one eye closed, and the stock of the gun braced against her shoulder as she took aim. The ball bearings hit the tins with a loud *tink* and they came tumbling down. She whooped, and I jumped up and down with excitement. The man behind the stall acted all impressed and presented her with a small brown teddy bear.

'A new friend for you,' she said, handing him over to me. I was a little too old for teddies – just a few months later and he would probably have gone to Carey – but that word *friend* resonated. And there was something about his face, the sad little brown eyes, the dot of a nose at the end of a blunt bear muzzle. Unlike most of my other toys, he didn't have a smiley face and I liked that. Who wants to be stuck with just one emotion all the time? I called him Kentucky because I liked the sound of the word and I decided, quite deliberately, to pretend he was alive. I pretended so hard that eventually he just was.

Kentucky spoke with a growly voice and a slight lisp. He climbed into my school bag and hid in my drawer all day, whispering silly things to make me giggle in class. I really did hear his voice – I can still remember it now better than I can my mum's.

He went everywhere with me, either openly under my arm or hidden in my backpack to avoid teasing from the other kids. And so he was with me the first time I met my funny friend.

Even as a super-naive seven-year-old, I knew something wasn't right with him. I could see the twitch in his left eye, the odd way his mouth twisted at the corners when he spoke, and the way he ran off whenever it looked like Mum was coming back. But he liked Kentucky. He went along with my fantasy completely, rather than in that patronising way most adults did, and so Kentucky liked him right back. Most of all, though, there was something about him which made me feel like I was the one in charge. That's a powerful feeling when you're seven years old, and I used to talk to him a lot about the way nobody understood how grown up I was, about the annoying things Mum and Carey did. Just little gripes, but it felt good to be listened to.

Like that day at the mall. School was on an INSET day, and instead of doing something fun we'd been trailing behind Mum all morning while she did errands. By the time we all paraded into Primark to look for pyjamas for Carey, Kentucky and I were royally pissed off. So when Mum wasn't looking, we just left.

I didn't go far – there was a stationery shop opposite jammed with colourful pens, pencils, sweet-smelling rubbers – just the sort of place Kentucky and I liked to browse in. I knew if I stayed in the front part of the shop, I could keep an eye on Mum and re-join her when she was done.

My funny friend showed up almost straight away. He smelled weird and his face was all shiny with sweat, but he seemed happy to join in with us, sniffing the scented pens I offered him. Even now those fake fruity smells make my stomach turn. As we played, I moaned about stupid Carey annoying me in the lift on the way up here, and stupid Mum always taking her side and how she was ruining my life by making me do boring things on my day off. I forgot to keep an eye on Primark until suddenly I felt a hand grab me roughly by the shoulders, pulling me away.

I saw the fear and panic in my friend's eyes before I turned around, and so I panicked too, wriggling to get away, thrashing around. I looked up and saw it was Mum, her fingers gripping me tightly. Then my fear turned to anger.

My friend was long gone, out into the mall and away and I felt sorry for him – how could Mum be so unfair? I wrenched my shoulders round out of Mum's grasp and turned on her, full of rage. I yelled horrible stuff, called her an evil witch, a nasty old cow.

I don't remember ever losing my temper like that before, but Mum didn't seem shocked, she just seemed tired and worn down. She grabbed my arm and Carey's hand, and dragged us back down to the car park. I did everything I could to make it difficult for her. I wriggled and screamed and sat down on the floor and, because I was doing it, Carey started screaming and crying too. Mum had to drag us along the shiny floor by our legs, then pull both of us into the lift.

By the time we got to the car, I'd fallen into a quiet, seething sulk, my jaw clamped tight, my eyes burning a hole in Mum's back. Mum pretty much shoved Carey into her seat and held her down by force to strap her in. Then she turned to me and I knew I was in for it. She grabbed my shoulders again, so hard it hurt.

She was almost shaking me, and cuddling me, and shaking and cuddling – shouting the whole time. Didn't I know *anything*? Didn't I know not to talk to strangers?

'Look at me, look at me, LOOK AT ME,' she shouted, and I wouldn't do it. I scrunched my eyes tight shut out of stubbornness, and fear too – I had never seen her this shaken up before. 'Stay away from that man,' she said, turning away with a groan of frustration, leaving me to clamber in by myself and going back to Carey's side of the car.

He must have followed us down from the mall, watched me screaming and fighting and hating my mother, because I caught sight of him nearby, and suddenly an idea sparked up in my brain: I knew how to fix this. Maybe he'd been getting it wrong, running and hiding every time he saw her – he had nothing to hide, after all. I would introduce him to Mum, she'd calm down and everything would be OK. I held up my hand, and beckoned him over. I didn't see the knife.

He killed them. Because of me.

I was still frozen from the shock when he rushed to my side of the car and tried to get me to go with him. He grasped my hand and pulled, told me there was a room in his house for me, a bed for Kentucky, that Mum and Carey couldn't hurt me any more. And wasn't I pleased? Wasn't it great?

I didn't answer him – terror and shock had shut my mind down – but I do remember him telling me he did it for me.

Afterwards, when the police pulled me out of the car, I couldn't speak. My throat was closed and my mouth was dry. I thought I might never speak again. I was too afraid of what my words could do. So I didn't tell the police that he had been my friend, that we'd hung out and made each other laugh, and that what happened was all my fault. Nobody from the stationery shop came forward. I guess kids have tantrums in there all the time and they never saw the connection. When Crow was arrested, I was terrified that he'd tell but he didn't. And so I kept quiet too.

I could never tell Dad it was my fault, watch him lose the one perfect daughter he had left. The shrink lady tried to get it out of me, but she would have wanted to make me better and stop me feeling this way. I didn't want to stop. I *wanted* to feel this way, I deserved it.

My last words to my mother and sister were filled with hate, and he killed them because of it. Neither of us deserves a future.

I've locked him in a garage on a derelict industrial estate. His phone is broken. Nobody will hear him screaming for help. The people at the party won't go looking for him – I could tell just by talking to them that they didn't give a crap. This isn't what I planned but it's still justice. He'll die of hunger and thirst and then he'll be gone, the link between us broken. I really don't care what happens to me after that. I'm just cardboard, a flimsy cut-out of a human being with no life, no identity. Once he's gone there'll be nothing left of me.

Chapter 31

Boyd, now

Oh shit oh shit oh shit. I'm kicking the walls and now the door of the garage, my feet slamming as I roar, pulse throbbing in my jugular, I can feel blood rushing through my body, thudding in my head and there's nothing, nothing I can do to escape. Worse than prison, worse than living with Tony. The others are long gone but I know what they would say: I fucking well deserve to die. I should have just sat there and let her stick the knife in me. Would she have killed me quickly? She doesn't look like the kind of person who knows where to stab but she knocked me down, didn't she? She might have had it in her. I should have let her try.

Instead I nearly beat her. All that prison time, all that worthy, learn-a-skill bullshit I bought into, and nothing changed who I am. I'm still the vicious, useless git I always was – a nasty piece of work.

Stay away from her, they told me afterwards. Don't think about her, she doesn't want to hear from you, she doesn't want to know anything about you. Shows what they know, those experts, because when I was lying in my bunk whispering to her, it turns out she was whispering right back.

After it happened, I did what I could to keep her safe. I never said a word about our friendship even when I was out of my mind right at the beginning. Never told the feds or even my defence lawyer anything about her at all. I didn't even talk to the shrinks they sent. The defence, the prosecution, I couldn't trust either side to keep her safe so I kept my mouth shut. Even when they implied all sorts of nasty, shitty stuff about why I hadn't harmed her: one piece of depravity they could never pin on me. It was never about that.

There wasn't one single moment when I understood what I'd done – it came in flashes, right from the start. The horrified look on her face; the feeling in my chest as I ran from the car park; that photo of three happy, smiling faces they showed on the news. Each flash of insight chipped away at the fake reality of Me-And-Golden-Girl-Against-The-World until I realised: I was a killer. I had smashed her life into pieces. Now the only thing I could do to protect her was to keep her away from me.

It took the prison shrinks a while to figure out what was going on with my brain, to give me the right cocktail of drugs to drive the others out and get me calm again. She was the reason I let them tinker around in my head. I got clean and took my meds so if I got out I wouldn't ever find myself getting weak and going back to see her. And I managed it – shipwrecked in this town full of strangers, I built a flimsy shelter, something like a life.

Then she comes to my door instead, still golden but with a hard sheen over her eyes that I put there and a question she's been asking herself for years. This was my chance to let her off the hook, shoulder the blame like I should. And what did I do? I made her feel like it was her fault. Some fucking protector I am.

Anyway, it's bullshit. All those years I told myself what I did was for her, but it was Tony's face I saw when it happened. That knife was meant for him. I picked on the weak, just like the prosecution said, like the papers said afterwards, and all those little old ladies who called the phone-in shows wanting me dead.

And now what, now she is gone and all's quiet and I have nothing but a locked door, half a can of Coke and no friends, nobody coming to help. This is when I finally think of them – the brave mother with her angry voice and fighting spirit, who didn't hesitate to chase off a gangster to defend her daughter. I think about that little girl with her dimples and bright eyes who should be growing up now. Blame the drugs, blame the gang, blame the broken home, blame the others – but the knife was in *my* hands.

And now here it is again – the same knife, heavy and familiar in my grip even after all these years. I wonder if she left it on purpose because it's completely clear what I have to do.

Chapter 32

Ellie

I had been afraid to move throughout Leah's story. I'd stayed sitting on the hard bathroom floor staring up at her. But now I dragged my stiff body up onto my feet and hugged her. It felt natural this time and she relaxed into me, her arms fitted around my back. She was warm, trembling slightly and little dry sobs broke the rhythm of her breath. I never felt so useless in my life. Nothing I could say would take this pain away from her.

I released my arms and she stood up, staggering slightly after being perched on the bath for so long. In the twin room it still felt like night time as the rain continued. Outside we could hear cars splashing past, commuters rushing through the downpour to the station, a train pulling away. The sounds of normal life.

Leah unwrapped her hands. The bleeding had stopped and bruises were starting to form. Her fingers moved stiffly but they could at least move, and we bound them up in strips of an old T-shirt she had with her.

Then, just as Mum would have done, I made us each a cup of tea and we sipped it, eating custard creams out of little packets.

'I'm ready to go home now,' she said.

I nodded. Home sounded good to me, even if it was the shop, and even if we had a lot of explaining to do.

Quietly we started pulling our things into our bags, Leah still fragile as a dry twig and shaking. I tried to tell myself that things would work out OK. That somebody would find Crow and let him out, and he wouldn't die of hunger and thirst, cold and alone. It wasn't my responsibility. I had found Leah and was bringing her home – wasn't that enough?

I pictured us getting on the train, each mile taking us further away from this place, the estate, that stupid party, that isolated garage, until none of it was real any more.

It wouldn't work.

Even if we did it: I got Leah home, we talked our way out of it, patched things up with Mum and David and went back to organising the wedding . . . There would be a report on the TV, a headline on my newsfeed. What's that phrase they use? *Found Dead.*

Someone would be dead because of us. Because I let us walk away.

As for Leah, every day after that would add another layer to the tight ball of guilt and tension inside her as she pretended to be perfect again.

She had come here because she wanted to stop waiting and change something and, somehow, I had to help her.

I sank down onto the bed and leaned forward, steeling myself to say the words.

'Leah,' I said. Her shoulders tensed, but she kept folding clothes neatly into that battered suitcase. 'Leah, you know

247

what I'm going to say – you've probably already thought it yourself. You know that your mum wouldn't have wanted this for you. And you know that your sister would not somehow feel better up in heaven knowing that you'd killed a man – or even hurt him.'

The corner of her mouth tightened slightly, lips pressed together, holding in another sob. Back in the days before, when there were rules about talking to Leah, I would have stopped there. But a fat lot of good the rules had been, so I kept talking.

'Seriously, not one thing in this world will get better if we just leave him.'

'It might,' she said. 'What if he goes on to kill someone else?'

'You can't ever know that. Leah, what he did was disgusting and wrong and horrific, but you have to learn to live in the same world as him. You've got to let him be the bloke who fixes motorbikes. You know that really, it's why you ran away instead of hurting him.'

Ran away – the wrong words. Leah flinched at that.

I had hoped she'd be with me on this, that she'd realise how crazy it was by herself, but it was up to me to say it out loud.

'I'm sorry, Leah, we have to go back and let him out.'

Chapter 33

Leah

I am empty, my eyes dry and sore, mouth parched, walking beside Ellie on legs as delicate as straw. The throbbing in my hands has dulled now, only stabbing at me when I open or close my fingers.

The rain hasn't let up and the air feels heavy with water as we move through it. The B&B landlady has lent us umbrellas, but we're still soaked. As I walk my wet socks rub against the inner sole of my sneakers, making a squeak with each step. We don't talk, so all I can hear is the squeak, the patter of rain on my umbrella and the shooshing sound the downpour makes as it hits the leaves on the trees. The air smells sharp.

Why am I letting Ellie take over? Why did I tell her where the lock-up was? Because somehow overnight I have become flat and worn out and she has become the leader, the wiser one. I don't even care how humiliating that is right now, I just want someone else to make my decisions for me.

Nothing has changed at the industrial estate. It's still deserted, tangled up with weeds, a lake-like puddle forming in the middle of the car park. There's no sign of life at the lock-up except for a thin strip of light leaking from under the door, merging with the puddles outside. The padlock is still in place. Ellie splashes up to the door, cautiously, taps on the metal.

'Er . . .' I realise she's struggling to remember which name to use, so I tell her in a whisper. 'Sam? Are you still in there, are you all right?'

There's a grunt from inside, an affirmative.

'I'm Leah's stepsister – I've got her here. We want to get you out, we want to help but I'm scared, OK? I don't know you and you're probably pretty angry right now, but could we just let you out and forget what happened before? Leah's sorry.'

'I'm not,' I say without thinking, and get an exasperated look from Ellie. But as I speak the words, I'm filling up with new strength again – different from before. Dropping my umbrella, I take a step forward, resting my forehead on the cool steel.

'I'm not sorry, I'm confused. I thought it would help me to hurt you, but it didn't. But if you want to attack someone when you come out, save it for me, not Ellie. I don't want anyone else getting hurt because of me. Even you.' These suddenly feel like the truest words I've spoken for years.

Another sound comes from inside. A choke. A sob.

Ellie's expression changes from fear to panic. She's looking down and suddenly I can see Crow's fingers poking out from a crack under the door. I look at those fingers – pink and vulnerable, resting in the rainwater. I could touch them, or I could crush them but I can't will myself to do either. I kneel down, my head must be level with his on the other side of the door, and my knees are soaked.

'It wasn't you,' his ragged voice comes from inside. 'I . . . I was the one . . .' He talks but it doesn't make much sense – about someone called Tony, someone called Kyle, someone he'd lost and let down. He gives a strange kind of grunt, a sharp intake of breath. And then silence.

I stand, shake the door in exasperation causing the metal to rumble.

'Crow?'

The fingers are curled upwards now, gripping the door tightly, and a dark red liquid is spreading out beneath them, flowing into the puddle like a curl of scarlet smoke. I feel a rising horror as I realise what it is, what he's done.

'I'm trying to do the right thing now,' he says. 'For both of us.'

Chapter 34

Ellie

Oh hell. I grabbed Leah's shoulder, tugging her back and throwing her off balance as I kicked at the door. The puddle was red with blood, but it wasn't a flood. It was a deep ruby red – rich and shiny. It gave me hope, made me think he hadn't severed an artery.

'Crow – Sam – are you OK? Tell me. The door's padlocked from the outside but we don't have the key. Is it in there with you? Can you push it out under the door?'

Nothing. I screamed in frustration, gave the door another kick and the adrenalin from that gave me a burst of energy. My brain churned over and over with different solutions.

'Right, Leah – run. I'm going to call an ambulance and you shouldn't be here. Go back to the B&B, grab the bags and I'll keep you posted.'

Leah looked like she was made of paper, about to dissolve away, but she shook her head weakly. She knelt back down and, to my amazement, touched Crow's fingers.

'I don't want this,' she said, as if she was discovering something new. 'Crow, don't do this.'

Another sob came from inside and the fingers disappeared. I unlocked my phone and dialled 999.

Then, with a surge of joy I saw something – a piece of bright metal slowly scraping through the crack under the door. The padlock key. Leah grabbed it, fingers slipping as she turned it in the lock.

As the door swung upwards, Crow crumpled forward into the puddle – a bundle wrapped up in an old army coat. Next to him lay the knife, wicked and polished but sticky with blood. Crow had pushed up his sleeve. He'd made a dozen tiny cuts on his left arm – it looked like he'd been working on them all night. Then there was one big savage one at his wrist, blood still oozing from it. Distant memories of first aid classes came back to me, of giggling in the back with Billie and wondering if I'd ever remember all this stuff.

'Take your jumper off,' I ordered Leah. I knew I was supposed to make a tourniquet but I didn't trust myself to do it right, so I bunched up Leah's top and compressed it against the wound, holding his arm up so it was elevated but resting against my legs. Rain soaked the knees of my jeans. Crow didn't resist me, didn't even speak. He faced away from me, staring glassily at the garage ceiling, conscious but not talking.

Leah crouched next to him, staring down at his helpless eyes.

I waved my phone at her. 'Just talk to the operator,' I said. 'Tell them where we are.'

Leah murmured into the phone and I stayed curled over Crow's arm, taking in every detail – every graze, every pale hair and the faint traces of a tattoo long since lasered away.

This man who was a killer was soft to the touch, his breathing ragged and sharp, and there was no fight in him.

The flashing lights bounced blue off his pale skin, the sound of ambulance wheels crunching on debris, doors slamming, paramedics' boots on the ground. I looked over my shoulder and saw Leah on the chair in the corner of the garage, head in her hands.

'Are you a relative?' the paramedics asked, as I stepped back for them to do their work. 'Do you know his next of kin?'

I was still fumbling around trying to answer their questions when the police arrived, and I realised the unholy amount of trouble we were in.

Chapter 35

Leah

I don't think Dad has hugged me this hard in years. His arms are tight around my shoulders, his fingers claw at me, digging into the plasticky softness of Ellie's jacket as if he's trying to absorb me into himself. And I relax into it, letting a flood of comfort and relief swamp me as I feel the soft texture of his fleece on my cheek, smell a faint trace of the aftershave Claire bought for him. At the back of my mind there's an echo of an alternative future – one where he's staring at me through bars, with a look on his face that I'm glad I will never have to see in real life.

'Oh Leah, oh Leah,' he sobs. And again, 'Oh Leah,' as if the relief has robbed him of his usual wise, fatherly words. I open my eyes and see that Ellie is getting a similar crushing treatment from her mother. She catches my eye and we share a knowing look. There is going to be yelling later, so best enjoy this while we can.

Once Dad lets go, he slips his hand into Claire's and there's something easier and more unconscious about the way he does it which makes me realise they've cleared the air. I hope that Dad's started talking to her honestly, that Claire will stop tiptoeing around him, that maybe we all have a chance. I will make him apologise to Ellie later, that will be a start.

I'll also tell them the full story – including what just happened, here in the police station.

In the hours after we left the lock-up, all I could see whenever I closed my eyes was his blood, shiny and red, so much of it. I could sense that we were in the back of the police car, I could hear Ellie trying to talk us out of trouble by claiming that we were 'just passing and heard a shout'. But I couldn't handle it. I couldn't work it out – everything was overlaid with a flow of red, twisting and curling into a grubby puddle.

I hated Crow. I would never stop hating him, could never forgive him for my mother's quiet gasp, for Carey's one little cry, no matter how many times people explained his mental illness, his troubled background. But the moment I saw that blood, I knew I didn't want him dead. When I heard Ellie tell the ambulance crew that he had no next of kin, I actually felt *sorry* for him.

I am sure this is supposed to make me feel like I am growing as a person, but in truth it could just be that I'm a disgusting coward, a failure. I could argue that it's a better punishment for him to live every day in wretched unhappiness, tormented by the guilt at what he's done, but that's bullshit. I just don't want anyone else to die, not even him.

I went along, limbs weak and limp, feet plodding, as the officers deftly separated us and put us into grey, box-like rooms. Mine had a chipped, dirt-coloured table and three cheap plastic chairs inside, a collection of dull informative posters on the wall and dusty blobs of Blu-tack clinging in square shapes, the ghosts of old flyers. Their talk of social workers and legal guardians was a muffled hum to me, the weak tea they gave me didn't even feel wet in my mouth.

An officer came in, the stab vest she was wearing making her look even more bosomy than she was. The seams of her uniform were straining and she seemed slightly out of breath. Ellie's voice piped up in my head, telling me not to be such a snooty cow, and after that I could see she had a calm, authoritative face buried in amid all the safety equipment. She drew back the chair next to me with a scrape and sat down, her body language deliberately friendly, making it clear this wasn't a formal procedure.

She told me that Crow was out of danger. 'He also told us the knife we found was his,' she said. For a couple of moments, she was silent, letting the words sink in and encouraging me to wonder *why would she tell me this, unless she knew he was lying?*

'He's very grateful to you for calling help when you did,' she continued in a slow, deliberate tone. 'He wanted us to say thank you before we let you go home.'

I spoke without thinking. 'Is he in trouble?'

She explained that he was on licence, that his supervising officer would be contacted. I knew that his parole prevented him from making contact with either me or Dad, that having a knife – and not just any knife but *the* knife – could be a ticket back to prison. I also knew now that prison would crush him.

Why would he do that for me? I felt a surge of absolute rage at him for taking my power again, for making any sense of justice feel muddy and confusing, rather than clean, swift and simple. Whether he was doing it through kindness, guilt or pity, I didn't know. I only understood that his actions bound us together again, even more tightly than before. And there was only one way to break away. I had to tell them the knife was mine.

The blurred, fuzzy feeling slipped away as I looked up at the officer and told her, quietly and calmly, that I'd like to make a statement.

Chapter 36

Ellie, one year later

Mum was stressing about the carpet in the hallway. She was on her hands and knees wearing bright green rubber gloves and aiming a spray-gun of Vanish at a stubborn cat-pee stain on the grey wool. The room was so thick with air freshener I could taste it on my tongue.

'It's not coming out,' she said again. 'I can still smell it.'

We'd been living in the semi-detached on Barton Avenue for six months now and the lady who'd lived here before, and her thirty-five cats, were still haunting us. But no matter how many fleas we found in Dylan's rug, or what that mysterious stain on my bedroom wall really was, it was still better than the shop. Because it was ours – mine, Mum's, Dylan's, David's and Leah's. From the moment we moved in things felt brighter.

Oh, there were fireworks after our seaside trip, endless rows over who was to blame, where we'd gone wrong, why-didn't-you-tell-us, yada yada. David and Leah talked *a lot*, and he haunted the house for weeks with such a hopeless expression of failure on his face that I felt truly sorry for him. But Leah worked at it, trotting along to therapy like an angel, enough to convince the authorities not to prosecute her for the knife. To start the process of setting her free.

And now here we were, a normal, bickering family with everyday stresses – like our less-than-perfect flooring.

'It's fine,' I lied, kneeling down next to her to inspect the spot.'We can live with it until the laminate comes next month.'

Mum's shoulders sagged, and then I realised why she wanted it gone now and laughed. 'Come on Mum, he's not going to care about that, he's a *bloke*.'

Mum opened her mouth to reply, but then jumped at the sound of a key in the lock. Making a strangled cry about rubber gloves, she fled into the kitchen before the door opened.

And so it was that Leah came home for the first time in three months to find me on my knees before her.

'Oh really, there's no need,' she said, waving me to my feet and laughing.

Whatever witty retort I had half-formed faded away at the sight of her. She was tanned. Not just the kind of tan you get on holiday, but the comfortable deep sheen you get from living somewhere sunny and just walking around. There were dashes of sunshine in her shoulder-length hair put there by the weather, although the streak of cyan at the front was the work of a colourist with serious skills. Despite the hot day she was still wearing that awful brown fleece. It seemed to fit her more now – she had curves and seemed even taller than before.

But the weirdest thing of all was the boy standing next to her with his arm linked in hers, smiling and holding out his other hand for me to shake.

I'd seen him on Skype a few times, but I hadn't been prepared for the full-on wave of gorgeousness and charisma crashing over me. My mouth gaped open, and a slow smile spread over Leah's face. Oh, she was really enjoying this moment.

'Ellie, João – João, Ellie.'

I rehearsed the pronunciation in my head: *j-WOW*.

At this point, Mum breezed in, gloveless and looking totally in control of the situation, ushering them through to the kitchen, where the IKEA table had been laid out with a selection of Brazilian treats she'd researched online and painstakingly made. Most of them involved sugar and condensed milk, which was fine by me.

As Mum fussed around, I noticed Leah's hand reach out and take João's, just giving it a little squeeze before letting it go, and I felt a rush of emotion, the feeling that this was exactly how it should be, which nearly brought tears to my eyes.

It's the same way I felt when Josh and I had a particularly satisfying play-fight before collapsing, breathless with laughter on the floor next to each other. It just felt right.

'Why's she grinning like that?' Leah asked.

'That's Ellie's Josh-face,' Dylan said. He and Leah exchanged a knowing look. 'Quick, change the subject or she'll start going on about him again.'

I popped something delicious and deep fried into my mouth and resisted the urge to re-tell the story everyone had heard a million times. About how Guy-from-the-party had found me online, how we'd chatted about YouTube and parties and mad things we'd done until finally he'd said, *I've got a mate who'd be perfect for you. He's a film-maker too . . .*

'I know, I know,' I said. 'But it's just nice to find someone who respects the things you like and doesn't want to change you. Someone who really gets you.'

Dylan groaned loudly, but Leah smiled.

'Yes. It is.'

Just then the back door opened and David came in, hands grubby with earth and cheeks pink from the effort of digging. He looked up, saw Leah and I just had time to duck out of the way as he flew towards her, folding her in a huge hug. Her arms came around him too and squeezed tight.

'Brazil is too far away,' he said, his voice muffled by her shoulder, hair and fleece.

'Oh, Dad,' she whispered, so quietly that I strained to hear. 'I love it.'

You can imagine how hard it was to convince David that Leah needed to take a gap year, even though her therapist supported the idea.

Eventually Mum pointed out that keeping Leah close and involving her in the charity hadn't really worked, and he gave in. And so off she went to the land of rainforests and capoeira, exploring a lush, beautiful country, doing her martial arts and hanging out with incredibly hot Brazilian men. Yeah, I could see why that was working better than therapy.

After fighting Dylan for the choicest sweet snacks, I found an excuse to slip upstairs for a few quiet moments. Thumbing through my emails I saw a short message from Boyd. He's not big on writing but he checks in now and again and I filter some of the info through to Leah when the timing's right. It says he's surviving, he has a new probation officer and reckons he is finally getting the help he needs.

No time to reply now, though, I had to get today's vlog done or I'd lose the light.

My bedroom was just as much of a mess as the rest of the house. The wallpaper was the same – a hideous beige, fabric-plaster shade, covered in stains and splatters. The carpet had been so foul we'd rolled it up and thrown it away. But a week after we moved in, David had produced a pot of white paint and together we'd painted one corner of the room, decked it with fairy lights and dragged a vintage leather chair into it. My filming spot.

'I'll never understand what the point of this is.' David had shrugged as I fiddled around with a few props and set up the GoPro.

'Everyone needs a hobby, *Dave*,' I'd told him – he laughed, still mystified by What The Kids Get Up To These Days.

I had nothing big to say on the day of Leah's return, just news of my latest Asos haul and the revelation that I'd decided to go to law school (a career where you argue for a living and get paid a FORTUNE!) but it didn't matter that this was a quiet day. You still need to post regularly, or your fan base disappears, and I wouldn't want that.

After a few minutes of hair-tweaking and subtle contouring, I positioned myself in my bright corner, sparking up the fairy lights and hitting record.

There was no glitter, not any more. But as the red light blinked on, I grabbed my shiny green apple and took a huge, satisfying bite.